The Princess School

Beauty Is a Beast

Jane B. Mason ❧ Sarah Hines Stephens

SCHOLASTIC INC.

New York Toronto London Auckland Sydney
Mexico City New Delhi Hong Kong Buenos Aires

For Nora and Violet,
our own royal princesses in progress.

—JMB & SHS

Copyright © 2004 by Jane B. Mason and Sarah Hines Stephens.

All rights reserved.
Published by Scholastic Inc.
SCHOLASTIC and associated logos are trademarks
and/or registered trademarks of Scholastic Inc.

ISBN 0-439-56554-5

12 11 10 9 8 7 6 5 4 3 2 1   4 5 6 7 8 9/0

Printed in the U.S.A.   40

First printing, December 2004

Chapter One

Perfect Cage

Briar Rose stared at the fire crackling in the enormous hearthroom fireplace. The flames flickered and danced, warming the giant room. It might have looked cozy if it weren't for the tall woman pacing noiselessly in front of it. As usual, Madame Garabaldi was a formidable presence.

The instructor walked back and forth in a swirl of robes, pausing only to stare intently at the room full of Bloomers — first-year students at Princess School — sitting straight in their high-backed chairs. She seemed to be sizing the novice princesses up, and none of them dared to slouch or scratch or whisper. Rose felt the tension in the room grow with each pass. Normally Madame Garabaldi made the official Princess School proclamations immediately after scroll call. Today something was different. The usually stern teacher looked downright rigid.

On her seventh pass Madame Garabaldi finally

spoke. "The time has come to begin preparing in earnest for your Royal Midterm Exams, which shall take place next week. The marks you receive on these exams, your first official marks here at Princess School, will signify the beginning of your royal academic career. Do not underestimate the importance of this trial. Your performance on these exams will influence the course of your future at Princess School and beyond."

Was that all? Rose felt the tension drain from her shoulders. Marks and exams were nothing to get your petticoats in a bind over. She looked happily over at her friends Cinderella Brown, Snow White, and Rapunzel Arugula, expecting to have her relaxed smile returned. They did not look relieved in the least. Snow was pale, as always, and shivering slightly. Ella looked almost as wide-eyed and white as Snow. Even unflappable Rapunzel looked nervous as she chewed on the end of her ridiculously long braid. None of them could take her eyes off the teacher.

"I am sure you are all anticipating the most challenging portion of your Royal Exams." Madame Garabaldi had stopped pacing before the fire and now strolled quietly among the students. "I expect the Princesses Past and Present oral examination will prove difficult for many of you. The questions will not be easy, and it will be your initial foray into public speaking." The teacher stopped in front of Rose's desk. "For others it will be a trifle," she said more quietly.

Rose could feel Madame Garabaldi's gaze on her, along with the stares of half the princesses in class. She kept her chin high but her own eyes cast downward. This was the appropriate way for a princess to show both pride and humility.

Rose knew Madame Garabaldi was right. The exams would not prove difficult for her. When she was a tiny baby, seven fairies bestowed her with the gifts of wit, grace, and intelligence — among other things. Rose always did well at, well . . . everything.

The other girls in the classroom did not share Rose's confidence. She heard the worried whoosh of whispers start as soon as Madame Garabaldi uttered the words "oral examination." And in the silence that followed, many of the Bloomers were unable to stop their unflattering fidgeting. These princesses were royally stressed!

Rose tried again to catch the eyes of her friends as the trumpets sounded to mark the end of hearthroom. She stood and began to gather her things, as did the rest of the girls. But Madame Garabaldi held her hand at head height, palm facing out, and every girl retook her seat.

"From this moment on I expect all of you to devote as much time as possible to your studies. Do not take these exams lightly. The marks will be permanently sealed in your royal record." Madame Garabaldi dropped her hand, releasing the girls.

The Bloomers hurried into the large marble corridors, toward the velvet-lined trunks where they kept their scrolls and texts. There wasn't much time before the next class since Madame Garabaldi had held them past trumpet. Rose overheard snippets of exam talk as she made her way through the crowd to her friends.

"If we fail, are we permanently dismissed from school?" one girl asked.

"I don't know," another replied. "I heard a bad mark meant you could never be coronated. Failures are transferred to a school for ladies-in-waiting!"

Several Bloomers gasped, and Rose hid a smile behind her hand. She knew for certain that *that* wasn't true, because her own mother had done poorly in more than one of her classes at Princess School. And now she was a queen! Rose knew her fellow first-years were big worriers, but they were also smart, and they had plenty of time to prepare. There really was no reason to fuss.

Rose scanned the crowd for Snow, Ella, and Rapunzel. She felt sure her friends would feel more confident than the rest of the Bloomers. But when she caught a glimpse of Snow and Ella, the two girls had their heads bent close together, and Ella had a worried look on her face.

A tense-looking Rapunzel waved Rose over. "Listen to this," Rapunzel whispered and nodded toward Ella.

"She said so just last night at dinner." Ella gulped. Her eyes looked damp.

"Maybe she was joking," Snow said hopefully.

"My stepmother doesn't joke," Ella said sadly.

Rose gave Rapunzel a questioning look.

"That rat Kastrid." Rapunzel shook her head sharply and had to put up a hand to steady her towering hair. "She told Ella that it's up to her to make sure her lousy stepsisters do well on their exams. If those two empty-headed snakes get bad marks, Kastrid will hold Ella responsible."

"But Hagatha and Prunilla are third-year Robes!" Rose gasped.

"I don't know how I will have time to help them and study for my own tests," Ella said. She blinked several times, fast. "Everyone says these exams are going to be hard!"

"Regally hard," Snow said worriedly. Rapunzel nodded in silent agreement.

Rose suddenly felt badly for not realizing how anxious her friends would be about the upcoming exams. And for not having to worry herself. Perhaps being bestowed with fairy gifts wasn't so terrible after all.

Putting her arm around Ella, Rose searched for the

perfect thing to say. "Don't worry, you can do it even if they are regally hard. You can do anything. You're the hardest worker I know." Ella didn't look at all convinced and even Rapunzel gave Rose a skeptical look.

"Easy for you to say," Rapunzel said. "I mean, the exams won't be regally hard for *you*, right?"

Rose grimaced. She knew Rapunzel was right — she didn't have to worry about exams as much as the other Bloomers did. But that didn't make her concern for Ella any less genuine. Rose opened her mouth, but before she could say anything three short trumpet blasts rang through the hallway.

"Oh!" Snow cried, grabbing Rose's hand and pulling her toward the Stitchery chamber. "We'll be late!"

As the four friends tumbled into the classroom, Rose felt the stares of the other Bloomers already in their seats. More than one looked at Rose with open admiration, and Rose felt her stomach clench.

It's not me they admire, she thought with a jolt. *It's the fairies' gifts.*

As the Bloomers watched Rose take her seat, she felt their admiration and expectations press in on her. She felt stifled, trapped in a cage of perfection. And suddenly, more than anything, Rose wanted to break free.

Chapter Two
A Perfect Mess

Rose's needle darted in and out of the taut muslin. Her mind was racing as quickly as her thread, and she was glad that she did not have to pay close attention to what she was doing. All she wanted to think about was the tangle of feelings she'd been having. But her reflections were interrupted by hushed conversation behind her left ear.

"Oh, they're going to be terrible!" a high-pitched voice whined. "I wish we could get our servants to take them for us. Exams are so hard!"

"Not for everyone," another voice put in. The princess spoke so quietly Rose had to strain to hear. "I bet they'll be a cinch for Beauty."

Rose cringed at the mention of her nickname. Did everyone think because she had gifts she didn't have troubles? Or fears? Or feelings? Being "perfect" wasn't all pearls and crowns! Rose always had to do exactly what other people expected her to do. What about what *she* wanted to do?

Annoyed, Rose accidentally pushed her needle through the fabric in the wrong spot. *See, I'm not completely perfect,* Rose grumped as she started to take out the misstitch. Hadn't she just messed up her needlepoint? Rose stared at the botched job, and suddenly the idea that had been rippling in her head became as clear and still as the waters of a wishing well.

Instead of fixing the bad stitch, she jabbed the needle through in another wrong spot, then another. How was that for perfect? Maybe if people didn't always know what to expect from her they would not expect so much!

Rose took bigger and faster and sloppier stitches. She chose new garish colors and inserted them in crazy crosses. She made snags and knots and then held her hoop at arm's length to admire the mayhem. She stifled a giggle. It was hideous!

"Lovely, girls. Lovely!" Madame Taffeta cooed from her desk. She brought her slender hands together three times. "Now it is time to display our work for all to admire. Please hang your embroidery hoops by the window so the natural light can enhance their comeliness."

Rose glanced back down at her creation and felt a twinge of guilt. She had purposely done the assignment wrong. What would her teacher and parents and fairies think?

Rose set her lips firmly. What about what *she* thought? Didn't that count? Why did she always have to live up to everyone else's expectations? The guilty feeling vanished as quickly as it had arrived. It was forced out of Rose by a new feeling — an exhilarating feeling — the thrill of making her own choice.

With a bounce in her step, Rose walked to the front of the room and hung her hoop in front of a sun-drenched window. She knew no one could possibly admire her work. It was not dainty, or delicate, or beautiful. And it certainly wasn't perfect!

When the girls were back in their seats, Madame Taffeta strolled slowly past the hoops. "Very nice, Ariel. A bit smaller stitches, please, Rapunzel. Lovely color choices, Ella. And oh —"

The teacher stopped short, staring openmouthed at Rose's work.

Rose bit the inside of her lip, waiting for the teacher to cry out in horror. But she didn't. Madame Taffeta just stood for several long moments, staring. "Briar Rose, is this *yours*?" she asked finally.

"Yes, Madame," Rose answered proudly.

"It's . . . it's . . ." Madame Taffeta struggled with the words. Curious, a few of the Bloomers got out of their seats to peer over the instructor's shoulders. Even Rapunzel got up. But while most of the girls let their mouths gape open in stunned silence, Rapunzel turned to Rose and mouthed, "Wow!"

"It's . . . perfectly stunning!" Madame Taffeta finally exclaimed, making several of the girls jump. "It's utterly magnificent!" She whirled around to beam at Rose. "Positively avant-garde!" the teacher squealed.

"I love it," Ariel, a petite Bloomer with flowing red hair, said to the princess next to her. "It reminds me of the sea."

Several other Bloomers nodded in agreement. A second later the whole chamber was abuzz with praise for Rose's needlepoint. Only Ella, Snow, and Rapunzel were silent.

"Magnificent!"

"My father would buy it for his collection!"

"I think it's refreshing."

Now it was Rose's turn to let her mouth fall open. This was hardly the reaction she'd expected. Even when she tried to botch it, everyone still thought her work was perfect!

The trumpet sounded. A dazed Rose let Ella, Rapunzel, and Snow lead her to lunch. At first none of them said anything. Then Snow finally spoke. "I'm so sorry," she said to Rose, her dark eyes even wider than usual. "I thought the needlepoint was interesting, but not nearly as pretty as your usual stitching."

Rose nodded. She completely agreed with Snow. How could Madame Taffeta have liked the mess she'd made?

I'll just have to try harder if I want to prove that I'm not perfect, Rose thought.

During lunch Rose slurped her squash soup as inelegantly as possible while she listened to Ella outline her plan for helping Hag and Prune.

"I can quiz them on Royal History while I'm helping them dress in the morning," Ella said. "And if I can write out questions while I prepare the dinner, I'll test them again at night when they get ready for bed."

"The dwarves always sing songs when they tuck me in," Snow offered. "Maybe you could sing Hag and Prune the answers."

"I won't have time to think up songs," Ella said. "It will be enough work just to learn all of their questions and their answers!" Ella sighed. "Even if I can learn the third-year curriculum myself, teaching it to Hagatha and Prunilla is going to be practically impossible."

"I'd sure like to teach them a thing or two." Rapunzel glared across the enormous room at the table where Hag and Prune were eating. Thanks to Ella, their gowns were beautifully cleaned and pressed, but even their perfectly starched collars couldn't hide the sour looks on their faces.

Rose wiped her mouth on her sleeve. Gazing at the yellow soup stain on her arm, she smiled to herself. She would show the world she was more than just a pretty face — starting with a few more sloppy bites.

Chapter Three

The Pleasure Is Yours

The Princess School doors opened with a soft *whoosh* and Rapunzel stepped out into the afternoon sunshine. It felt as great to finish a day of school as it did to begin one. And today there was a handsome prince waiting for her at the end of the Princess School bridge — her pal Prince Valerian.

"Val!" Rapunzel called, running up to him. Val was a second-year student at The Charm School for Boys. He and Rapunzel had been best friends since Val had stumbled upon Rapunzel's tower four years earlier. He'd dared her to scale down the outside of the tower, and she had. Now she was looking forward to telling Val about Rose's creative needlepoint, and the crazy tangled hairdo Rose had invented after lunch in Looking Glass class. Val loved Rapunzel's stories about Princess School — and hearing about Briar Rose, too.

Rapunzel had almost reached her friend when another prince — one she didn't know — suddenly appeared next to him. At least his head did. He was standing on the far side of Val and must have been bending down looking at the swans.

"Rapunzel, this is my new friend Dap," Val said, gesturing to the hazel-eyed boy beside him.

Dap grinned and leaned forward to take Rapunzel's hand. "Nice to mee —"

Dap's long leg caught on the edge of a bridge rail and he fell forward, nearly crashing into Rapunzel.

"Steady there, Dap," Rapunzel said with a laugh, lending him her arm for support. "No need to swoon for me."

Dap laughed heartily as he straightened up. He was very tall — almost a whole head taller than Val. "You're right, Val," he said. "She isn't your average princess."

"She was raised by a witch," Val explained. "For real."

"A powerful witch," Rapunzel added proudly. "And she's getting to be a pretty good cook, too."

Just then Snow and Ella descended the school's front steps in a swarm of princesses. Rapunzel could just make out snippets of their conversation over the din of exam talk.

"Golly, what a day," Snow was saying as they crossed the bridge. "My head is positively spinning with all of the hullabaloo over the exams. I think it's even gotten to Rose. Jiminy, I've never seen her so flustered! Did you see what she did to her hair during Looking Glass class?"

Val stepped forward as the girls approached. "Snow White, Ella Brown, meet Dap," Val said with a flourishing hand.

"Dap what?" Ella asked.

"Just Dap," Dap said. But Rapunzel noticed that his cheeks had reddened.

Dap bowed and nearly tripped on a loose bridge plank, but saved himself at the last second.

Snow giggled. "Nice to meet you, Dap." She curtsied sweetly.

"And nice to meet you," Dap replied. "Val has told me all about you. But didn't you mention another princess?"

Out of the corner of her eye, Rapunzel caught sight of a decidedly imperfect tangle of hair — Rose. Rose had ratted her usually silky smooth, honey-colored hair in Looking Glass, creating an incredible mess . . . and quite a stir.

Rapunzel rather liked the new 'do. Since her own impossibly long locks were usually in a tangle of their own, she could relate. But she hadn't expected the response of the other Bloomers in class.

They weren't able to re-create Rose's messy hairstyle exactly, but as Rapunzel watched the crowd of girls descend the Princess School steps, she saw that they had certainly tried.

Rapunzel waved to her friend. "Rose! Over here!" she called.

A ratty-haired, rumpled, and cross-looking Rose strode over the bridge. Rapunzel smiled at the sight of her. She definitely looked different!

"Rose?" Val said, obviously surprised by the girl's appearance.

Dap stepped forward with unusually perfect ease. "Ahhh, *Beauty*," he said, emphasizing the name and smiling broadly. "Your reputation precedes you, but it hardly does you justice. You are indeed a perfect flower, Rose. It is my pleasure to make your acquaintance."

Rapunzel watched Rose stiffen. Her usually friendly blue eyes flashed as they sized up this gangly newcomer. Her smudged, soup-stained face contorted into a scowl.

"Indeed, the pleasure *is* yours," Rose snapped as Dap bowed to kiss her hand. "Because it certainly isn't mine."

Ella's hand flew up to her mouth in shock, and Snow gasped aloud. Dap simply looked stunned. Rapunzel was surprised, too. She knew Rose was having a difficult day, but she was always a polite and poised princess.

Rapunzel thought she saw a look of triumph flash across Rose's face, but couldn't be sure because it was gone in an instant. Rose was snatching back her hand to bat away a swarm of birds or large bugs or . . . no. It was Rose's flying fairy entourage.

The fairies twittered around Rose's head, tugging at her ratty hair and swiping at the dirt on her cheeks.

"Leave me alone," Rose muttered, batting the fairies away with her hand. She turned and, without so much as a wave to her friends, stomped off toward her father's gilded coach. The velvet-lined door closed with a loud slam and the horses bolted forward. A moment later, Rose was gone in a cloud of dust.

Rapunzel turned to Ella and Snow and saw that her friends looked just as shocked as she felt.

"What was that about?" Val asked.

"I didn't mean to upset her," Dap said, pushing a lock of his strawberry-blond hair out of his eyes. "I was only teasing. I just wasn't expecting the famous Beauty to be so . . . so . . ."

Val cringed. "I should have warned you, Dap. She doesn't like to be called Beauty."

"But I've never seen it make her . . . angry," Snow said, her hands at her chin. "She kind of reminds me of one of the dwarves," she babbled. "Only Gruff is really very sweet!"

"So is Rose," Ella pointed out.

"At least the *old* Rose," Rapunzel murmured. She really liked the creative streak Rose had been showing in school all day, but she couldn't believe how rude her friend had been to Dap. What had gotten into her?

"I'm sure she'll be in a better mood tomorrow," Ella said. "Unlike my stepmother, who's never in a good mood. Please excuse me, Dap — I'd better get home before I get in trouble for being late. Kastrid will cook my goose!" Ella waved to her friends as she hurried toward the lane that led to her father's manor.

"Oooh, goose!" said Snow. "Maybe I'll surprise the dwarves with gooseberry pies for dessert tonight!" Snow forgot her worries in an instant, skipped to the end of the bridge, and turned down her own forest path. Rapunzel was about to try to explain things to Dap when Val took her elbow.

"See you tomorrow, Dap," Val said as he led Rapunzel away. Dap waved, looking a little confused to have been so rapidly abandoned. Rapunzel thought she should invite him along, but sensed Val wanted to talk to her alone.

He probably wants to grill me about Rose, she thought. Val *always* wanted to talk about Rose.

"You won't believe this," Val said as soon as they were in the privacy of the forest.

"Believe what?" Rapunzel asked, secretly relieved that Val had some exciting news.

Val picked up a rock and skipped it into a nearby stream. "Dap's full name. It's William *Dapper*."

Val stopped and looked at Rapunzel meaningfully, but Rapunzel was silent.

"So?" she finally asked.

"Don't tell me you've never heard of the Dapper family!" Val said incredulously.

Rapunzel looked at him out of the corners of her eyes and moved ahead on the path. No, she hadn't. So what?

Val's jaw dropped. "Where have you been? Locked in a tower or something?"

That did it. Rapunzel turned and elbowed her friend in the stomach, getting a satisfying *ooof* for her efforts.

"Okay, okay!" Val said, holding up his hands in surrender. "The Dappers are a famous family of smooth socialites, known for their theatrical ways — especially their amazing masquerades." Val paused for effect, his eyes shining. "They just moved to our part of the kingdom. And they're throwing a masquerade party this weekend to introduce themselves to their new community! All the royalty in the land are invited, and everyone has to arrive in costume."

"Wow!" Rapunzel's eyes were shining now, too. A party! With costumes! It would be the perfect break from the stress of studying for the midterm exams.

Val's face suddenly grew serious. "Please don't let on to Dap that I told you, though," he said. "He asked

19

me not to tell anyone his last name. He doesn't like people to know who his family is."

"My lips are sealed," Rapunzel agreed. She could relate to Dap's plight. If his family was really a group of smooth socialites, she guessed the awkward prince didn't necessarily fit in. It was a little like being raised by a witch — something Rapunzel wasn't always anxious to reveal when she met new people. Sometimes it was nice to make your own impression.

Chapter Four
In a Dither

Rose's royal coach zoomed up to a large, sparkling castle.

"Whoa," the coachman called as he pulled on the horses' reins.

Rising out of her seat, Rose flung open the door before the coachman could get to it. She was anxious to get to her room. It had been such a strange day and she had a lot to think about. Only it was impossible to hear her own thoughts with her fairies flitting all over her.

"Watch your step, dear." Daisy fluttered by her ear as Buttercup and Viola tried to take her scrolls and textbooks.

"I can get out of a coach myself and carry my own things," Rose said flatly. The fairies' tiny faces looked crushed as they darted out of the vehicle. Rose immediately felt guilty for her harsh tone. But she was just so tired of being doted on!

With a sigh, Rose stepped out of the coach and walked up the drive.

"Good afternoon, m'lady, pixies," the butler, Godfrey, greeted them as he opened the door. His eyebrows shot up above his spectacles when he got a look at the resident princess. But he said nothing about her new hairdo as he closed the door softly behind her.

Rose lifted her skirts and hurried up the stairs. She could hear the buzzing wings of her fairies behind her, but they were keeping a distance. They were hurt. Rose couldn't blame them, but she couldn't bring herself to apologize to them, either.

Rose pushed open the carved mahogany door to her room with her shoulder and carried her things to her four-poster bed. The door closed behind her with a satisfying slam. Alone at last, she climbed up onto her fluffy down quilt and opened *Princesses Past and Present: A Primer*. No matter what her peers thought, she still had to study — at least a little.

Rose began to skim a chapter on Princess Paisley, a young girl who let a gnome talk her into selling her baby brother for eternal beauty. But her encounter with Dap kept playing in her mind. What was it he had said? Her reputation preceded her?

Not my *reputation*, Rose thought, *Beauty's reputation. And I never chose to be Beauty, either.*

It seemed no matter what she did, everyone thought

she was perfect. *I'll have to try harder,* Rose thought. *It appears a perfect reputation will take a while to live down.*

She turned back to her studies, but a moment later she was distracted by the beating wings and whispers of her fairies. They had flown into her room through her windows and were hovering by the curtains.

"Her father is going to have a spell," Buttercup said fretfully.

Petunia wrung her tiny hands. "That hair! It looks like a trampled field of wheat!"

"And look at her gown. Dahlia might have to use magic to get those stains out!" Pansy proclaimed. Unable to keep their distance any longer, the fairies buzzed closer. "Please, dear, tell us what happened. Who did this to you?" Pansy pleaded.

"I did," Rose said plainly. "I did it myself."

"Oh, no, dear!" Viola could not believe it. "Who are you protecting?" She darted in to try and untangle one of the knots by Rose's ear. Behind Rose, Buttercup and Petunia worked to smooth the rattiest part of her hair.

"Really." Rose had to laugh. She knew it was torture for her fairies to see her like this, and there were so many of them she could not fend them off. But she *could* excuse herself for dinner.

Rose made her way to the dining room, her fairies fluttering around her trying to finish their work.

"This strand won't behave!" Daisy exclaimed as she tried in vain to tuck it into Rose's braid.

The entourage hovered until Rose took her seat at the large square table in the dining room and Godfrey placed a delicate monogrammed napkin in her lap. The pale pink embroidery spelled BR.

"How was school today, dar —?" Her mother's gaze settled on Rose's hair and she stopped short. "What happened to your hair?" she asked, clearly alarmed.

Rose hid a smile as she put her hand up to her head. At least her family and fairies were noticing the new her.

"Is Madame Spiegel making you use hot irons again in Looking Glass? Oh, darling, I do wish you would let the fairies accompany you to school," Rose's mother fretted.

"Hot irons?" Rose's father, King Hector, cried. His bushy eyebrows clustered together in the middle of his forehead. "That sounds dangerous!"

"We're not using hot irons right now." Rose sighed. "I did this hairdo myself." Her parents seemed not to hear her. She'd hoped that going to Princess School would show them that life was not as treacherous as they thought. So far it hadn't. They were still as overprotective as ever.

"And anyway, Father, hot irons have been used to style hair for centuries. They're perfectly safe."

"I'd feel more comfortable if you'd just wear those gloves I purchased for you last summer," King Hector replied.

"Father, they're gauntlets! They're for dueling knights! I don't even think Headmistress Bathilde would allow them at school."

King Hector spooned some bouillon into his mouth. "You know how delicate you are, my flower," he said gravely.

Rose grimaced. She was *not* delicate. Couldn't her father see that?

Rose's mother, Queen Margaret, cleared her throat quietly. Rose knew she was anxious to let the topic drop. She was probably worried that altercations at the dinner table would upset Rose's appetite. "How was school today, darling?" she asked serenely.

Rose sighed. "Fine, I suppose. All the princesses are talking about is the midterm exams. My friends are really worried, and everyone is telling me how lucky I am that I don't have to worry, too."

"Isn't that nice." Queen Margaret smiled.

"Well, not really," Rose said honestly. She didn't usually tell her parents the whole truth when it came to how she was feeling. She didn't like to upset *them* at dinner, either — but this was the new Rose. "Everyone thinks it must be so easy to be me because of all the fairy gifts. They always expect me to be perfect. Well, it's not easy to have to be perfect." Rose was surprised by how fast she was talking. It all came rushing out.

"But darling, you simply *are* perfect," King Hector proclaimed. "You're the most perfect princess in the land!"

Rose stifled a groan and stared at the croutons floating in her consommé. She loved her father, but sometimes he just didn't understand.

"You are a special girl with special gifts," her mother chimed in. She put her hand over Rose's and gave it a little squeeze.

Rose smiled weakly. So much for telling the truth. Her family and her fairies just didn't seem to be able to hear it.

"We got an interesting invitation today," Queen Margaret said, changing the subject. "It arrived by page and was printed on remarkably bright blue parchment." She leaned forward, clearly excited by the delivery. "And the news inside was as startling as the color. There's going to be a party this weekend at the Dappers' new castle!"

King Hector clanged his silver spoon in his soup bowl. "*The* Dappers?" he said. "New castle?"

Rose's mother smiled and nodded. "Indeed. They have moved to our land and are throwing a masquerade! Rose darling, your name was on the invitation, too!"

Rose shivered with excitement. Her parents had attended several masquerades over the years, but she had always been too little to go along. This time she was on the guest list!

King Hector dabbed his eyes with his napkin. "Our perfect little angel is growing up," he said, taking the queen's hand.

Rose barely heard him. Her mind raced. She was thrilled to be invited to an adult party, but more than that, a masquerade was an opportunity for her to reinvent herself — her looks, her charms, her voice . . . everything. In costume, she could escape her reputation. She could be anyone!

There was just one question Rose needed to answer. Who did she want to be?

Chapter Five
Rats' Nests

Ella rinsed the last platter and set it on the counter next to the sink.

"Thank goodness," she told Bo, the cat. He was curled up in front of the hearth, but opened one eye to show that he had heard. Ella was glad to finally be finished with the dishes. Her stepmother, Kastrid, always wanted several courses served at dinner, and each one had to be presented with just the right china and flatware. Doing the dishes often took over an hour, and then there was still the sweeping and straightening up to do.

When the kitchen was spotless, Ella finished the ironing. Then she climbed the main staircase to her stepmother's room.

"What took you so long?" Kastrid snapped. She was seated at her dressing table, combing her long red hair. "I wanted my hair combed before sunrise, so I had to do it myself."

"I was finishing the ironing," Ella said simply. "Hagatha and Prunilla both wanted freshly pressed petticoats for school tomorrow."

"Well, you were too slow at your work, as usual," Kastrid spat. "I can only hope you're not your usual slow self when you're quizzing your sisters on their schoolwork. It will be hard for a stupid girl like you to keep up with their answers." She smirked at Ella. "Now lay out my nightdress and be gone with you. I'm tired of your face already."

Ella bit her lower lip as she opened her stepmother's wardrobe. She wished for a moment that her father weren't traveling this week. Though he almost never stood up to his wife for the sake of his only daughter, the sight of his friendly face always helped Ella get through the evenings.

"Hurry up," Kastrid ordered.

Ella pulled a neatly folded nightdress from the wardrobe shelf and laid it on the bed. Then she silently left the room, closing the door behind her.

As she made her way down the hall, Ella rubbed her shoulder. It was sore from carrying the food-laden dinner platters in and out of the dining room. She knew she should do some mending — the sewing basket was overflowing with things that needed repair — or study for her own exams, but she was bone-tired. All she wanted was to fall into bed and curl up under the covers.

"I'll do the mending tomorrow night," she told herself as she opened the door that led to the attic stairs. But before she could even put a foot on the bottom step, she was stopped again.

"Cin-der-el-la," Hagatha said drolly. "We'd like a word, if you please."

Cinderella turned toward her stepsisters and almost laughed out loud. Hagatha and Prunilla had back-combed their hair into rats' nests, just like Rose! Only on them the hairdos looked right at home — enhancing their natural nasty looks.

Quickly hiding her smirk, Ella looked seriously at her sisters' pinched faces. "Is that a new style?" she said.

"Poor Ella. You're too dim to spot a trend, even when it's begun by one of your closest friends," Hagatha said.

"Just look at her limp hair." Prunilla pointed and laughed. Then she stepped closer to Ella. "Do you know how Beauty got that gorgeous yellow beauty mark on her chin today at lunch?"

On one hand, Ella was tempted to tell Hag and Prune that the spot was a splatter of soup and burst their bubble. On the other hand, she did not want to tell them anything! She wasn't sure herself what Rose was up to. She suspected it had absolutely nothing to do with trendsetting, but she wasn't about to reveal anything to her awful steps.

"I don't know," she said, which wasn't a total lie. "I think she was just distracted in Looking Glass today."

Hagatha lifted her chin and narrowed her eyes at Ella. She seemed just about to say something when Kastrid suddenly appeared behind them.

"Ella, why are you standing idle in the hall? You should be assisting your sisters with their studies. Don't forget, their performances are your responsibility," she said.

Ella shuddered, unwilling to think about what might happen to her if Hag and Prune's marks weren't good enough.

"But Mother, we're exhausted!" Hagatha complained.

Ella rolled her eyes. *From what?* she wondered. *A full day of lazing around doing nothing? Dragging combs backward through their hair?* It was a miracle Hagatha and Prunilla made it through a day at school.

"All right, darling," Kastrid said sweetly, stroking her daughter's arm. "Ella can quiz you while you recline in one of your bedrooms."

"In mine!" Hag shouted.

"No, mine!" Prune insisted.

"I said it first!" Hag whined.

"Girls, girls," Kastrid said smoothly. "There are several nights of tutoring ahead of you. You can trade off. First one room, then another."

"Fine," Hagatha huffed. "But we're starting with my room."

Prunilla didn't object, though she sniffed haughtily and flounced down the hall, her spiked hair waving in the air as she moved.

"Hurry up, slowpoke," Hagatha sneered at Ella before following her sister.

Ella hurried up the stairs to get the notes on Robe curriculum she'd copied that day. Fortunately not all Robes were nasty like her sisters, and she'd found a couple of girls who had been willing to share their texts and notes with her.

By the time she got to Hagatha's room, her sisters were wallowing in the giant bed like a pair of pigs in mud.

"Stoke the fire," Prunilla ordered as soon as Ella stepped through the door.

Ella added a log, sat down on a stool at the foot of the bed, and cracked a *Gown and Fancy Dress* text.

"What is the traditional undergarment worn with a thirteenth-century ball gown?" she asked.

Hag and Prune looked at Ella blankly.

"My feet are cold," Hagatha finally said. "Bring us a hot coal basket."

"What was the traditional width of a farthingale during the sixteenth century?" Ella asked before setting down the text to get the coal basket.

"What's a farthingale?" Hagatha whined through her nose.

"I think it's a kind of bird," Prunilla said.

Ella hid a small smile. "A farthingale is a kind of frame worn under a gown to make the skirt puff out just so." Hag and Prune clearly didn't know much about their Fancy Dress curriculum, even though they had a wardrobe full of lovely gowns, hoops, and petticoats themselves.

They're as lazy at school as they are at home, Ella thought. *How will I ever get them to learn this stuff?* She wished she could summon her fairy godmother to help with the task. But Lurlina worked in the administrative chambers at Princess School — she couldn't meddle with midterm matters without risking her job. Ella would have to struggle through the exam period on her own.

"I'm too tired to study," Prunilla complained.

"All right," Ella agreed, though Kastrid's threatening words echoed in her head. Getting her stepsisters to do well seemed truly impossible. "We'll begin again tomorrow."

Ella closed the heavy dress volume and left Hagatha and Prunilla snickering over their new 'dos.

33

They aren't so tired that they actually need to sleep, she thought bitterly as she made her way up to her tower only to reopen her steps' texts and fight sleep to read them. If she weren't prepared to quiz them in the morning while she helped them get dressed, Kastrid would have her head. Ella's own studies would just have to wait.

Chapter Six

The Sincerest Form of Flattery

Snow sang as she stepped lightly onto the drawbridge that led to the Princess School castle. Momentarily halting her step, she waved merrily to the swans swimming in the moat below. "Hi-ho!" she chirped. "Good morning!"

Ever since she'd heard about the masquerade the night before, Snow had been trying to think of the perfect costume to wear to the event. And just as she'd passed the wooden sign that pointed to town, she'd come up with the perfect idea. And she knew seven experts who could help her with every little detail!

"A hat, a belt, leather slippers . . ." She ticked off the things she would need on her pale fingers. "And oh! A beard!" She giggled.

Snow turned away from the swans and instantly forgot all about her costume. She stared at a cluster of second-year Sashes making its way across the bridge.

They looked just like normal princesses . . . except their hair was ratted into big piles, just like the tangle on Rose's head the day before!

"Oh, my!" Snow said to herself as she followed the girls up the polished marble steps. One of the girls, a redhead named Leona, had tangled her hair so well that Snow wondered if she'd ever get the snarls out. Just thinking about trying made Snow's scalp ache.

Whoosh! The Princess School doors opened for the girls. Snow stepped inside. . . .

And found herself surrounded by princesses with very ratted hair. Snow automatically put a hand to her head to make sure her own hair was still arranged neatly.

Picking her way through the princesses, Snow searched for her friends and tried not to stare. It wasn't easy. Some of the 'dos, like Hagatha's and Prunilla's, made Leona's locks look combed smooth!

"Snow!"

Snow breathed a sigh of relief when Ella grabbed her by the arm and pulled her to the side of a carved archway. Rapunzel was there, too, smirking at the sight of the other Princess School students.

"Can you believe it?" Ella asked, her green eyes wide.

"I think it's great," Rapunzel put in. "Compared to these girls, my hair looks perfectly coiffed!" She reached up and patted her unwieldy braid affectionately.

"This is terrible!" called a breathless voice behind them.

Snow turned and saw Rose, who was rushing up to them. "They all look just like me!"

Snow gazed openmouthed at her friend. The other princesses may have looked like Rose, but Rose didn't look a thing like herself. Her hair was the messiest of all. Her dress was rumpled and torn. And the scowl on her face was anything but beautiful.

"Did you meet a wolf on the way to school?" Snow asked worriedly, examining her friend for scratches and wounds.

Rose sighed. "No, I didn't. I just thought I'd try something different."

Snow didn't know what to say. She thought Rose looked . . . awful. The other girls were silent, too. And Ella looked a little shaken. Her eyes were fixed on Rose's worn dress. Snow's heart went out to her. Ella was forever attempting to hide her own threadbare gowns.

Snow was trying to think of something nice to say when Rapunzel's expression suddenly grew serious. She turned toward Rose.

"You know, you really upset Dap yesterday when you stormed off in a huff," she said. "You might have been having a bad day, but he had no way of knowing that. He was just trying to be friendly."

Rose bit her lip. "I know," she said. "But he was so annoying! 'Your reputation precedes you, but it hardly does you justice,'" she said, imitating him. "Who does he think he is?"

"He was only teasing, Rose," Ella said quietly. "And I thought he was kind of cute."

Snow giggled. "Me, too. He's . . . different. I wonder where his family is from. And where does he live?"

"In the new castle on top of Noble Hill," Rapunzel replied plainly. "And you know you shouldn't judge a person by his family."

"That's for sure," Snow agreed. "Why, if people judged me based on Malodora . . ." At the thought of her stepmother, the pale girl shuddered, unable to go on.

Rose wrinkled her nose. "Well, wherever he comes from, he's a royal pain."

Snow opened her mouth to protest, but just then, the trumpet sounded and the girls had to hurry off to hearthroom.

Snow tried to concentrate on Madame Garabaldi's morning proclamation, but she couldn't help being distracted. Something was going on with Rose. Why was she so touchy lately? And why was Rose coming to school looking like such a mess . . . on purpose?

Snow pondered Rose's new image all morning and still didn't have any insight when it was time for her favorite class, Frog ID.

We'll talk to her at lunch, Snow decided as she made her way to the Frog ID classroom. *And we can check up on Ella, too.*

Madame Bultad waddled to the chamber and immediately began a lecture about famous frog princes in preparation for the upcoming exams. Snow loved frogs, and the idea of being turned into one captivated her. Life as a hopping amphibian sounded fun! *And if I were a frog, I wouldn't have to take exams,* Snow realized with a flash of envy.

"The most famous frog prince is, of course, Archibald Amphibious, but he had several lesser-known contemporaries, including Ignatious Hoppings and the velvet-throated Finnigan Ribbit."

"Ribbit," Rapunzel repeated quietly, imitating the instructor's croaking voice. The Bloomer next to her began to giggle, and a couple of the caged frogs that lined the tall, diamond-paned windows croaked in response.

"Of course, Finnigan was famous for croaking even long after he became permanently human. You see, due to the strength of the curse upon him he was doomed to croak instead of speak whenever he became excited."

The giggling got louder as several girls laughed at the idea of a prince croaking instead of talking.

"I assure you, this was no laughing matter for a

prince trying to woo his princess," Madame Bultad said sternly. But the laughter only got louder as each princess imagined a prince croaking at her. The only girl not giggling, Snow noticed, was Rose. In fact, Rose looked quite serious, with her face scrunched up and her nose slightly raised in the air.

Madame Bultad looked at her students rather sternly. "This is essential review for your exam next week," she said. "Unless you would rather risk failing?"

The princesses stopped laughing immediately, and for a brief moment the room was completely quiet.

Then, "Ribbit!" a giant frog called out from inside his cage.

"Ribbit! Ribbit!" called out other frogs.

"They must be terribly excited!" Ella said. "They can't speak at all!"

The giggling started again, and this time even Madame Bultad looked amused. Snow sat back in her chair and closed her eyes. The melodious sound of the croaking mixed with the princesses' laughter rose up to the arched ceiling, making Snow smile.

But a moment later Snow's eyes flew wide open. A new sound was drowning out the others. A *snorting* sound.

Did someone let a pig loose in here? Snow wondered as she quickly scanned the room. She saw no signs of swine, but the sound must have been coming from *somewhere*.

Snow let her ears lead her eyes to the source of the noise, and she gasped. The horrible snorting was not coming from a frog or a pig, or any animal, for that matter. It was coming from Briar Rose!

Chapter Seven

An Early Departure

It only took a moment for the laughter and ribbitting to die down. The Frog ID class was entirely silent — except, of course, for Rose's impossibly loud snorts.

Rose was filled with glee as she let loose another wave of her newly invented laugh. She sounded just like a pig! It was the most inelegant snort Rose had ever heard. Surely it would show her classmates that she was far from perfect.

Rose was so focused on her new laugh that she hadn't noticed the silence. Or the way that Madame Bultad's flat face had contorted into a deep frown . . . until Ella nudged her. By then it was already too late.

Rose's snort echoed loudly through the high-ceilinged chamber. It was repugnant, full of wet, throaty reverberations and a deep bass undertone. When the sound died away, Madame Bultad cleared her throat and began her lecture once more.

"As I was saying, Finnigan's curse was no laughing matter and in the end it sealed his fate. He lost his true love when, upon bended knee, he asked his princess to "croak" instead of asking her to be his bride." Madame Bultad struggled to hold back a tear while the Bloomers struggled to hold back laughter.

Rose pictured the surprised look on Finnigan's princess's face and could not hold her amusement inside. She laughed her new snorting laugh — but stopped short when her snorts seemed to multiply in the air around her. Though Rose silenced her snorting snicker, the piggish sound echoed on. The other girls in the class were laughing just like Rose!

Rose did not know if she wanted to laugh along with them or cry. She couldn't even laugh like a pig without being admired and copied by everyone around her! Didn't the other princesses know how ridiculous their snorting sounded?

Rose watched the princesses heave and snort, half wishing she had never tested out her new laugh at all. A few of the princesses were practically falling out of their chairs. She looked beseechingly at her friends, who appeared to be as surprised as she was. Even Rapunzel seemed off guard.

At the front of the chamber, Madame Bultad attempted to call out over the din, to no avail. Rose watched the instructor hop onto her chair.

"Ladies!" she called. But Rose could barely hear her over the echoing grunts, and the other princesses appeared not to hear her at all.

Madame Bultad began to hop up and down, flapping her short arms in the air. She was obviously becoming more and more flustered, but that only made the princesses snort louder and louder.

Finally she wrote something on a scroll and summoned a page. The sight of the pointy-hatted squire quieted the chamber, but only enough for Madame Bultad to be heard.

"Briar Rose!" she croaked hoarsely. "You will remove yourself from my classroom this instant and report directly to Headmistress Bathilde! Your behavior is a perfect disgrace."

There wasn't a snort in the chamber as Rose got to her feet. The only sound Rose heard was the horrified gasp that escaped Snow's lips.

Perfect disgrace.

There's the P word again, Rose thought as she moved slowly toward the door where the page stood glumly, holding the scroll. But she had never heard the word spoken quite that way before — nor had she ever been spoken to so harshly. Rose's new laugh certainly had succeeded in getting Madame Bultad to react differently to her. Only Rose was not so sure she liked it.

The door closed behind Rose with a soft puff of air and she moved numbly down the corridor behind the page. She had no idea what to expect. Never before had she gotten in trouble. It was rare that any princess had to be asked to leave class, and Rose had never — not even in her worst thoughts — imagined having to report directly to the headmistress.

The page tapped so softly on Lady Bathilde's door that Rose could barely hear the noise. The door swung wide as soon as his small hand left it, and Rose saw Lady Bathilde sitting on the other side of the chamber. She looked calmly at Rose from the far side of her ornate mahogany desk.

"That will be all, Bartholomew," she said calmly when the page had given her the scroll. "Do come in, Rose." Rose wished she were the page as the headmistress gestured toward a tall, highly polished chair. It had no cushion and Rose winced slightly as she slid onto the hard seat.

"Now tell me, why has Madame Bultad sent you to see me?" Lady Bathilde ignored the scroll the page had given her. Her expression showed no sign of pleasure or disappointment, even as it momentarily settled on Rose's ratted hair. As Rose gazed down at her rumpled gown, she was filled with embarrassment.

Rose took a deep breath and explained how she

had disrupted class with her new laugh. Still the head-mistress's silvery eyes revealed nothing. Finally, Rose stopped speaking and sat staring at her hands.

The headmistress stood and walked around her desk. She lifted Rose's chin. Her fingers were as soft and cool as her gaze and even when she let her hand drop Rose was not tempted to look away. "The most important thing for any princess is to be herself," Lady Bathilde said.

"Only when we are our true selves can we be of value to our families, our friends, our school, our community, and most important, ourselves." The headmistress retook her seat. "It is up to you to put your best self forward, Rose. You owe it to yourself and to those around you to be the person you truly are inside."

Yes! Rose wanted to shout. *Yes, I want to be the person I am inside. I want people to see the person I am inside.* Rose bit her tongue so she would not start blubbering and pour out all of the feelings that were crashing around within her.

"People look to you to set an example, Briar Rose." Lady Bathilde caught Rose in her gaze once more. "Are you being true to yourself — to them?"

I'm trying, Rose thought, but she felt the bars of her cage closing around her once more. The weight of other people's expectations and her own desire to make other people happy fell heavily on her heart. Lady Bathilde did not understand. She just wanted Rose to go back to being perfect — just like the fairies, just like her family.

"You may go, Rose," the headmistress finally said.

Rose stood and stumbled toward the door. She felt as numb as she had when she stumbled in, and just as confused. Only one thing was clear: She did not want to be sent to see Lady Bathilde in her chambers again.

Chapter Eight
Princess Pact

"How long has she been in there? You don't think anything bad has happened, do you?" Snow bounced on her tiptoes.

Rapunzel put an arm on Snow's shoulder to stop her fidgeting and to keep her from bolting into the headmistress's chamber and making things worse. The girls had been waiting for Rose ever since their class let out.

"Don't worry so much. We're talking about Lady B, not Malodora," Rapunzel assured her.

"Thank goodness!" Snow exclaimed. "My step-mother would probably cast a terrible spell on poor Rose."

"Lady Bathilde doesn't practice witchcraft, and she is always fair." Rapunzel patted Snow on the back. "How bad could it be?"

"Pretty bad?" Ella said softly with a weak smile.

She was right. Disappointing someone you liked

48

had a way of feeling worse than disappointing someone you didn't.

But Rapunzel wasn't as worried about what Lady Bathilde was going to do to Rose as she was worried about what was going on with Rose in general. Rapunzel had been all for Rose's strange behavior when she thought it was just for fun. But it seemed that Rose's antics were fun for everyone *but* Rose. And now her behavior had landed her in trouble. Something was going on.

Just then the chamber door swept open and Briar Rose stepped out. Her friends rushed to meet her like a pack of oversized wingless fairies.

"Are you okay?" Snow asked, reaching up to smooth Rose's hair but then, seeming to think better of it, placing her palm on the girl's shoulder instead.

"What happened?" Ella took Rose's arm and started to lead her away from the large chamber door.

"You should have seen Madame Bultad trying to calm those frogs after you left. I think the poor hoppers thought they were doomed to be hog slop." Rapunzel smiled at Rose, hoping her friend would smile back. She didn't.

"Please don't fuss," was all Rose said.

The four girls made their way toward their trunks in a huddle. Rapunzel was waiting for Rose to say something more, but she was silent and sullen.

Finally Rapunzel couldn't take it. "Okay, we won't fuss, but we need some answers." Planting herself in front of Rose, she stopped her and looked into her clear blue eyes. "We need to know what's going on. Why are you acting so weird? Are you okay?"

Rose's expression was somewhere between growling and sobbing. "I'm fine!" she burst. "I'm just tired of having to be so perfect all the time! Can't I have a bad day?" Rose let her shoulders drop and softened her voice. "I feel like everyone expects so much more from me than they do from everyone else. When Gretel snorts like a pig, *she* doesn't get sent to see Lady Bathilde!"

Rapunzel nodded. It was true.

"Gretel can't help being piggish," Snow defended the girl softly.

"Yeah, have you seen her nose?" Rapunzel smiled.

"That's not the point. Maybe *I* can't help it if I'm not perfectly perfect all the time, either." Rose pushed past Rapunzel and started walking again. The other girls stayed with her.

"But don't your fairy gifts —" Ella started to say.

"I know I am gifted," Rose said, newly exasperated. "But just because I am blessed by fairies doesn't mean . . . well, it's just that that isn't all I am. Everyone thinks I am so perfect because of those gifts. Those gifts are the only things they see. They think I'm so great — but it's not me they adore. It's the gifts. Why can't people just like me for me?"

"Oh, but they do!" Snow gushed. "Just look how everyone wants to *be* like you." She gestured toward the halls where about half of the princesses in the school were wearing their hair heaped in tangled piles.

"Exactly! They can't even tell when I'm not acting perfect! All anyone can see when they look at me is 'Beauty.'" Rose wrinkled her nose when she spoke her nickname. "All anyone can accept from me is perfection."

"So you're trying to act as imperfect as possible just to prove them wrong?" Ella asked.

Rose let her breath out slowly. "I just have to find a way to let other people see past Beauty to the real me."

Rapunzel considered Rose's words for a moment. She understood why Rose needed the other girls at Princess School to see who she really was. But she felt pretty certain that ratty hair and a snorting laugh weren't the true Rose, either.

"Oh, I hope you won't get in trouble again." Snow started bouncing on her toes at the thought, and all three of the other girls put hands out to stop her.

"No." Rose finally smiled at her worried friends. "I'm not planning on getting called to Lady Bathilde's chambers ever again!"

"Good." Ella looked relieved and Snow slowed her bounce. Rapunzel was pleased to hear this as well. But she still had a feeling Rose's antics weren't a thing of the past.

"I just have to change my strategy. And I think I know the perfect place to leave Beauty behind — the Dappers' masquerade! I haven't come up with a costume yet, but it's going to be good. Nobody but nobody will know who I am and then they'll *have* to judge me for me!" Rose was beaming. In spite of her messy hair, she looked more like herself than she had in days.

"Nobody but nobody? I'll bet you I'll be able to tell who you are, costume or no." Rapunzel crossed her arms and smiled slyly.

"Me too," Ella agreed.

Snow was nodding vigorously and her eyes were sparkling with excitement. "I'm not so sure you'll know who I am, though. I thought of the perfect costume this morning. I'm going to be a —"

Rapunzel clamped her hand over Snow's mouth and put a finger to her lips. "I have an idea. Let's not tell one another what we're going to be. Let's see if we can all guess who we are when we get to the masquerade."

"It'll be a breeze to spot you." Rose nodded toward Rapunzel's towering hair.

"That's what you think." Rapunzel grinned. She

loved games and this had the potential to shape up into a good one! "Are you all up for the challenge?" She looked at the nodding girls. Their eyes were bright, there were smiles all around, and the trouble in Frog ID was forgotten before the next trumpet blast.

Chapter Nine
The Perfect Costume

Rose dipped her quill in ink and let the ebony liquid drip back into the cut-crystal bottle before dipping and dripping again. It was the second day in a row the Bloomers had been given time in hearthroom to prepare for exams. And it was the second day in a row Rose had spent the time trying to think up the best possible costume to wear to the masquerade. She had moved from historical figures to farm animals by way of garden flowers and still she was not sure what to be. *A cow? No. A pig? Well, I already have my snort down*, she thought.

Rose shifted in her seat at the memory of Lady Bathilde's cool, steady gaze. She hadn't used her new snort since Frog ID. She'd been staying out of trouble, or at least out of the headmistress's chambers like she had promised her friends she would. But she hadn't quite given up her new less-than-perfect self here at school.

As she pondered her imperfect image, Rose let a drop of ink splatter onto her lace cuff. *Would an artist make a good costume?* she wondered. She sketched herself in a painter's smock, with a small mask made to look like a palette, but it did not entirely cover the face. Back to the drawing board.

Looking up from her sketches, Rose watched the other Bloomers. Each and every one of them was wrapped up in exam preparations.

Two desks away, Ella hurriedly copied third-year notes from borrowed scrolls, underlining good quiz questions as she went. Beside her, Snow focused so hard on her *Princesses Past and Present* text that the tip of her tongue was peeking out of the corner of her mouth — a princess no-no. Even Rapunzel's face was pinched in concentration as she worked one of her thick braids into a four-strand weave. Rose wondered if they had started their costumes yet.

Beginning another sketch — of a minstrel this time — Rose kept one eye on Madame Garabaldi as she slipped softly between the students.

Moving down each aisle, Madame Garabaldi peered at the princesses' work. Spotting a mistake, she would point at it with one finger while evading it with her eyes — as if it pained her to see it. She never gave out answers. Those the girls could find on their own. She only indicated flaws.

Discreetly Madame Garabaldi caught Snow's eye and touched the corner of her own mouth as she walked past. The girl's pink tongue disappeared between her crimson lips. Her pale cheeks flushed.

At Ella's desk the teacher did not point out any mistakes, but she lingered a little longer than she had before the other girls and her expression changed almost imperceptibly as she read over her shoulder. Rose forgot her own troubles for a moment and felt a flash of panic for Ella. Would her friend get in trouble for neglecting her own studies in order to prepare her stepsisters? And even if Madame G. didn't lecture her, how would Ella ever pass her own exams if she spent all her time at home and in school learning the Robe curriculum? Rose wished she could do something to help Ella. But what? *Fat lot of good my gifts do in a situation like this*, she thought helplessly. She was relieved when Madame Garabaldi moved on from Ella's desk without saying a word.

Madame Garabaldi swept past Rapunzel and was nearly on to the next girl when her gloved fingers materialized before Rapunzel's face holding an impossibly long, wayward strand of hair. With a puff of exasperation, Rapunzel snatched the strand and began her weave again. Rose flashed Rapunzel a quick grin and went back to her drawing.

Even when a shadow fell across her sketches, Rose

did not look up. She was lost in a daydream, drawing costumed figures dancing around the edges of her parchment. She imagined kings, queens, princes, and princesses hidden behind masks, asking her one question: "And who might you be?"

The single cluck of a disapproving tongue made Rose jump. Madame Garabaldi towered over her desk. Her eyebrows were raised and she looked about to say something, but her lips never moved. She swept on.

Rose let out her breath. She was relieved not to get a lecture, or worse. She also felt something else — disappointment. Why hadn't she been told to study? Evidently not even the strictest instructor in the school thought Rose could deliver a less-than-perfect exam. Rose was certain that any other Bloomer caught sketching instead of studying would have faced severe reprimands. "Beauty's gifts will get me by," Rose said softly to herself. The thought was bittersweet.

Rose let a drop of ink fall on the parchment and watched it bleed out into the fibers. It looked like hair, and suddenly Rose was pulled back to her costume fantasy. She stared as the furry dot spread, a beastly blemish on the otherwise perfect parchment.

At last she had it — the best idea of all. She would not be a cow, or a painter, or a pig. Rose would be the furthest thing from a beauty she could think of. She would be a beast!

Chapter Ten
Working Ahead and Falling Behind

Ella bent her head low over her scroll and continued writing as quickly as she could. Her hand ached from writing all period, but hearthroom was the only time she had to copy the notes she needed for quizzing Hag and Prune that night. Her steps were too lazy to take notes themselves, and the Robe who'd lent Ella her notes needed them to study for her exam, too!

Never mind my own studies, Ella thought grimly.

A single trumpet blast signaled the end of class. Ella wasn't quite finished, so she skimmed the remaining paragraph about Queen Pretensia and her awful son, Horrace. The boy was as lazy as Hagatha and Prunilla combined.

Ella gathered up the scrolls and texts and hurried into the hall. That was the second study period she'd had to spend entirely on her stepsisters' curriculum. And between quizzing the terrible pair and doing her chores at home, there wasn't a second left over for her to review her own material. She hadn't done a stitch of work on her costume for the masquerade, either!

At least she had an idea of what she wanted to wear. A good one, she thought. If she could only stay awake after tonight's tutoring session, she might be able to get it done. But first she needed to find some feathers.

Ella's golden suede slippers padded softly on the pink-and-white stone floor as she rushed down the hall toward the Robes' velvet-lined trunks.

"Thanks so much, Tiffany," she said breathlessly as she handed the pile of note-taking scrolls back to their owner.

Tiffany smiled warmly. "Sure," she replied. Then she leaned forward slightly. "But I'm doing it for you, not your sisters."

Ella smiled back, then scurried away. She was almost to her classroom when she ran into her friends. They were all smiling broadly. Ella knew right away that something was brewing.

"Rapunzel has an idea to help you get your step-sisters ready for —" Snow was cut off by Rapunzel, who was jerking her head in a very unroyal manner. Ella turned and saw Hagatha and Prunilla swaggering down the corridor.

"Your beauty secrets are truly inspired, Rose," Rapunzel said loudly.

Ella shot Rapunzel a surprised look. Since when did she care about beauty secrets?

Rose gave Ella a quick wink. "Oh, not really, Rapunzel," she replied in a raised voice. "They come right out of that book Ella is holding."

"Really?" Rapunzel put her hand to her chest in mock surprise. "You mean to learn all your beauty secrets I would only have to memorize that book?"

"Absolutely," Rose affirmed. "But please, don't tell anyone else."

Within half a second Hagatha and Prunilla had pounced on Ella, snatching the book from her hands.

"Give me that!" Hagatha hissed.

"Gladly," Ella said, trying to hide her smile. The book was *Gowns and Fancy Dress*! But Hag and Prune were such lousy students, they didn't even recognize their own textbook.

"I had it first!" Prunilla screeched, trying to pull the book away from Hagatha as the two girls made their way down the hall cackling like a pair of jackals that had happened upon a feast.

When Hag and Prune were out of sight, the four friends burst into laughter.

"That was brilliant! Rapunzel, you're a genius!" Ella

beamed at her friends, grateful for their help. "Thank you so much!" she said, giving them a hug.

"You're welcome," Rapunzel replied, her eyes bright with excitement.

Snow led the way down the corridor.

"Come on," she said. "We've got to get to history class."

The girls rushed into the chamber and took their seats. On either side of Ella, princesses had already opened their texts to the chapter called "Decorum Through the Middle Ages." Ella quickly flipped to the appropriate page, which showed several princesses in severe-looking undergarments.

"The proper princess attire of the twelfth century was rather, er, elaborate," Madame Istoria said. "But a princess would not consider leaving even her bed-chamber without being fully dressed."

"Look at those stays!" one of the girls exclaimed, pointing to an illustration of a dark-haired princess in a stiff whalebone corset.

Snow giggled. "Positively primeval!"

Ella gazed down at the image in front of her. Indeed, the young girl looked terribly uncomfortable. "It was what the princesses wore over their dainties that *really* made things uncomfortable. There were so many layers that many princesses swooned from the weight alone. Once upon a time most royal families had servants whose only responsibility was to get the family dressed and undressed!"

At the front of the room, Madame Istoria looked up, surprised. "Someone's been reading ahead!" She beamed.

Ella blushed at the teacher's compliment.

Well, if I'm behind in the Bloomer curriculum, at least I know the Robes'! she thought. Ella sat up straighter and willed herself to pay close attention to the exam review lecture. This might be the only review she got before the midterm! But she was just so tired . . .

By the time the final trumpet sounded, Ella's feet felt like lead. She was so weary she could barely make it to her trunk, and for the first time all year she wished she could ride home in the coach with her stepsisters, even if it meant she'd have to be in their company for the duration of the trip. Of course they'd never let her. Ella always walked to and from school.

"You look exhausted, Ella," Rapunzel said as the girls gathered their cloaks, texts, and scrolls. "Do you want Val and me to walk you home?"

Ella stifled a yawn and nodded. "That would be great," she said. "That way I won't fall asleep under a tree on my way."

"Oh, Nod does that all the time," Snow said as she

closed her trunk. "He just dozes off anywhere! Why, just last night he fell asleep in his bowl of soup!"

Ella giggled as she, Rapunzel, and Snow started for the door. Snow was always ready with a good dwarf story.

"Where's Rose?" Ella asked, looking around. She was so tired she hadn't noticed the girl's absence before.

"She dashed off right after the final trumpet," Rapunzel said. "She said something about getting to work on her costume."

"Ooooh!" Snow cried. "I've been gathering everything I need to make a perfect —"

"Shhhh!" Ella and Rapunzel said together.

"It's supposed to be a secret, remember?" Ella reminded her.

Snow clamped a hand over her own mouth and nodded several times, her brown eyes as wide as saucers.

The girls headed out into the autumn sunshine. Still holding her hand over her mouth to keep her secret safe inside, Snow waved good-bye and skipped off over the bridge. Rapunzel linked her arm through Ella's and led her worn-out friend to the tree where Dap and Val were waiting. Ella felt instantly cheered at the sight of the two boys. Val was always great to have around — and Ella looked forward to getting to know his new friend Dap.

"We're walking Ella home," Rapunzel informed the boys.

"Our pleasure," Val said, bowing gallantly.

"Certainly," Dap agreed.

The four crossed the bridge and started down the path to Ella's father's manor.

"How's your costume coming, Ella?" Rapunzel asked.

Ella stepped gingerly around Dap, who was holding a wayward tree branch aside for them to pass. "I have an idea, bu —"

"Ooof!" Dap tripped on a large oak root and let go of the branch he was holding, nearly knocking the girls off the path altogether.

"Nice one, Dap," Rapunzel teased as Dap got to his feet. "Is that a new jousting move?"

"The path is treacherous here," Val defended his friend. "And Dap has never been on it before."

Ella smiled. Val was a good friend and had a good point.

Dap cleared his throat. "Never mind, Val. They're on to me. I'm as clumsy as I am tall," he admitted with a laugh. "But we were talking about the lady's costume for the masquerade." Once again he moved the tree branch aside, letting Rapunzel pass.

Ella giggled. She had to admit that Dap was charming in an unusual sort of way — a lot more charming than she'd first thought. And he was funny, too.

"As I was saying earlier, I have an idea, but no time to get to it. Kastrid has me quizzing Hag and Prune for their exams every second I'm not doing house chores." Ella let out a frustrated sigh.

"Why don't you let us help you with something?" Rapunzel suggested as they approached the wrought-iron gate surrounding Ella's father's estate. "Maybe I could quiz your evil steps for you."

Ella recognized the mischievous look in Rapunzel's eye. "No thanks," she replied with a smile. Playing an exam preparation trick on her nasty stepsisters would be great . . . until they failed and she got in trouble for it. "But you could help me with another project," she said.

Rapunzel, Dap, and Val all stood attentively on the path, waiting for instructions. Ella was overwhelmed by their willingness to do anything she asked. Her friends — even her newest one — were truly wonderful.

"I need as many feathers as you can get from the aviary and the henhouse," she explained. "Can you gather them up and leave them next to the back door by the kitchen?"

"Of course, m'lady," Val said with a grin.

And with a curtsy and a pair of bows — one with a stumble — the threesome headed off toward the coop.

Chapter Eleven
A Beast in the Making

Rose drummed her delicate fingers on the curved-legged writing desk in her bedroom. Her school scrolls and texts lay on the glass top, but Rose had pushed them aside almost immediately after taking them out. It was her pale pink sketching scroll that held her attention.

Her charcoal skimmed over the parchment, adding sweeping lines and tiny details to her sketch. Rose was designing her beast costume for the masquerade and was almost finished. Soon she would be ready to begin building her creation!

Rose held her sketch at arm's length for a better view. "Perfect!" she said. Then she stuck out her tongue at the word she had uttered without thinking. "I mean, beastly!" She smiled to herself.

A soft buzzing echoed behind her and a moment later Rose's entourage of fairies engulfed her.

"Ooooh!" Petunia shrieked, hovering over Rose's sketch. "How dreadful."

"What an unattractive creature," Dahlia agreed.

"What is it?" Tulip asked simply.

"And why on earth have you drawn it on your lovely parchment?" Viola wanted to know.

"It's a beast!" Rose replied proudly. "My costume for the masquerade."

"Oh, no, dear!" Pansy cried. "You can't go to the party dressed as such an ugly creature. I'm sure everyone expects you to go as something beautiful and wonderful, like a butterfly or a unicorn."

"Well, everyone is going to have to adjust their expectations, then," Rose replied. "Because I'm not going as something beautiful. I've decided to be a beast."

Pansy and Tulip eased the parchment out of Rose's hands. Rose was tempted to clench the sketch tighter, but decided against it. There was no use getting the fairies into a fuss. Besides, she was so thrilled by their reactions to her costume that she suddenly didn't mind humoring them . . . for a bit.

"Would you like some help with your studying, dear?" Daisy asked. She cocked her head to the side.

Viola tugged on the end of a scroll, her wings beating frantically with the effort. "We can quiz you, if you like."

"You're certain to do well, but it's always good to be prepared," Tulip coaxed.

Rose knew the fairies were right. It *was* always good to be prepared. But right now she was too excited about her costume to study. Besides, there were still several days before exams. She had plenty of time.

"I've already studied today — at school," she fibbed. Rose felt a twinge of guilt as soon as the words were out of her mouth. She had never told a lie to her fairies — not even a little white one. She was debating whether to correct herself when there was a light knock on the door.

A housemaid poked her head into Rose's room. "Dinner is served," she said.

Rose got to her feet and followed the servant to the dining room. The dinner was perfectly prepared, as usual, but Rose had no appetite. She dragged her silver fork across the porcelain plate but did not bring it to her lips.

"Are you fretting about midterm exams, my precious?" Queen Margaret asked.

Rose shrugged slightly but didn't say anything.

"Don't let it worry your pretty head!" her father boomed. "I'm certain you'll do just fine." He reached over and patted his daughter's hand.

"Everyone is," Rose said sulkily. But if her parents heard her, they didn't show it.

"Why, Rose, are you slouching?" her mother said, sounding truly surprised. "Slouching is so unattractive. It's just not you. Are you feeling all right, darling?"

When I'm a beast I'm going to slouch all night long, Rose thought. And suddenly another moment at the table acting like the daughter her parents expected her to be seemed like torture. She had to escape and get to work on her costume right away. But first she would need to collect the right materials.

"Daddy, may I have one of your old fur coats?" she asked.

King Hector nodded absentmindedly. "Of course, my Rose," he said. "But I would happily buy you a new sable of your own. Something tawny to offset your lovely hair perhaps?"

"That's very generous, Father, but not necessary. Your old fur will do." Rose quickly forked up a token bite of meat. "May I be excused?" she asked.

"You've barely eaten," her mother said. She looked sympathetically at her daughter. "But I suppose it's difficult to have an appetite with exams approaching. You may go, but don't study too hard, dearest."

Rose smirked. "I won't," she promised. She pushed back her chair so forcefully her father looked up from his roast beef.

Rose lifted her skirts and ran all the way to the wardrobe that held her father's old furs. After sifting through several, she found a thick brown one with several moth holes. Perfect.

Rose carried the heavy fur to her room and set to work. First she cut long strips off of the front of the coat and sewed the now-narrower coat closed. Then she stitched the back and front together, making a kind of fur pantsuit. She had to use a large needle and embroidery floss, and it was slow sewing. Pushing each stitch through took some doing, and for once Rose was grateful for the thick thimbles her parents insisted she wear on the tips of her fingers when doing needlework at home.

As she tied off a piece of thread, Rose wondered what her friends would be wearing to the masquerade. Would they recognize her when she was dressed like a beast? Were they working on their own costumes?

Poor Ella, Rose thought. How would her friend manage to find the time to make her own costume with all the extra exam preparation she had to do?

Rose eyed the study scrolls sitting untouched on her desk and felt a fresh wave of guilt about neglecting her own studies. She hadn't exactly lied to her parents at dinner, but almost. That was two lies in a single evening.

Rose brushed a smear of glue onto a gold-trimmed mask she had found in a trunk in the stables and pressed a piece of fur onto it. As she reached for a second piece, Lady Bathilde's words echoed in her head.

"You owe it to yourself and to those around you to be the person you truly are inside."

Am I being true? Rose asked herself. Part of her thought she was. She was doing something she wanted to do — that was being true to herself. But another part of her wasn't so sure. She felt terrible about lying, even though it had gotten her what she wanted. And she knew she should be studying. The exams were just two days after the masquerade. Even though school came easily to her, Rose had always been diligent in her schoolwork. Doing her best had always been important to her. At least until now.

"I'll do a little bit of review as soon as I finish my costume," she said aloud as she fixed another piece of fur to the mask. "Even if I don't do my best, I'm sure it will be good enough."

Chapter Twelve

Fowl Play

Rapunzel picked up the egg-gathering basket outside the door and bent down to step into the chicken coop. The ceiling was even lower than the one in Snow's cottage!

"Cluck, cluck, clucker!" the hens inside greeted Rapunzel, Val, and Dap as Rapunzel's eyes adjusted to the dim light.

"Wow, Ella's father is serious about chickens," Val said. "There are a lot of hens in here." It was true. Two entire walls of the coop had built-in nesting compartments, and nearly every one had an egg lying inside.

Dap reached for the basket Rapunzel was holding. "I'll gather a few egg —"

Thunk! Dap whacked his head on one of the low rafters.

Rapunzel hid a smile as she handed over the basket. Then she and Val began to gather soft white feathers from around the coop.

"Ouch!" Dap exclaimed as he bonked his head a second time. He dropped an egg on the coop floor and the slippery insides oozed out the cracks.

"Anyone for scrambled eggs?" he asked cheerfully, rubbing his head.

Rapunzel laughed out loud and picked up several tail feathers from an empty cubby. "No thanks, I prefer them poached." She was liking Dap more and more, and was glad Val had a friend at Charm.

In spite of his mishaps, Dap's egg basket was just about full, and Rapunzel's pockets were stuffed with feathers. "On to the aviary?" Val asked. "There's quite a bit of vertical clearance there," he added.

"Thank goodness," Dap breathed, rubbing his head.

Rapunzel squinted in the sunlight and led the boys down the garden path to the aviary. Ella's father had a fondness for birds and had built a large enclosure for them to live in — complete with a pond. There were several species — everything from peacocks to parakeets, toucans to chickadees.

Rapunzel led the way inside. Dap had to duck slightly to get through the door, but once inside was free to stand tall.

"Look at this!" Rapunzel exclaimed as she picked up a tail feather. There were several lying nearby, so she gathered those up as well.

"I wonder what Ella needs all these feathers for,"

Val mused as he plucked a small feather up off a stone near the pond.

"Maybe Kastrid wants a feather boa," Dap suggested.

"I'd like to give her a boa of a different kind," Rapunzel said with a scowl. "One that's constricting. That woman treats Ella like dirt."

As she gathered up the last few loose feathers, Rapunzel guessed that the plumes had something to do with the masquerade. She suddenly felt a little lame for not having come up with her own costume idea yet. If Ella — the busiest girl she knew — could think of an idea, she should be able to, too.

"Let's get these back to the manor," Val said. He had turned his cloak into a makeshift hammock and stuffed his feathers inside. Several renegade plumes were sticking out the gaps in the side. "Maybe if Ella can show Kastrid that she has finished her tasks early, she can get a moment to herself."

The three carried their collection back to the manor house and left them at the back door.

"I hope that's enough," Dap said as they turned to leave.

"That's all there was!" Val said. "I think we got every last feather."

Rapunzel was uncharacteristically silent as she followed behind the boys, considering costumes. What should she be? A witch?

I'm sure Madame Gothel would be willing to lend me a robe and a spell or two, she thought. *But what if someone mistakes me for a real Grimm girl?* Rapunzel shuddered. The witches who attended the Grimm School were just that — grim.

Rapunzel shook her head. No, a witch wouldn't do. The witches and warlocks weren't invited to the masquerade, and it would be terrible to be kicked out because of a convincing costume.

"I know!" she said suddenly, snapping her fingers. She turned to Val. "I need to come over and borrow some stuff," she told him.

Val crossed his arms across his chest. "What are you after, Rapunzel?" He narrowed his eyes suspiciously.

"I only require a few items of clothing," Rapunzel said innocently. "Would you deny a fair maiden?"

"You've always envied my breeches!" Val teased. "But don't think dressing like a prince will get you into Charm School."

Rapunzel grinned. "I hadn't thought of that," she said slowly with a knuckle under her chin. "But I'll take the breeches and a tunic . . . and maybe a helmet."

Chapter Thirteen
Hide and Go Seek

"Ah-choo!" Rose sneezed as she pulled the furry hood and face mask over her head. Squinting through the eyeholes, she stepped back to look at herself in the tall, gold-framed mirror. She could hardly believe the day of the masquerade had finally arrived. Nor could she believe the hideous effect her costume had now that it was finished. It was truly terrible!

Rose took a long look at her reflection. With the shabby, fur-covered gardening boots and the yellowed teeth and claws she had attached to mouth and paws, she was every bit a beast. There was not a scrap of "Beauty" showing through. She'd even rubbed sap and tar into the fur of her father's old coat to make it look matted.

"Did I hear a sneeze?" Petunia called from the corridor.

"You shouldn't be rushing off to a party if you're becoming ill," Buttercup added nervously as she buzzed into the room. She fluttered up to Rose and swooned at the sight before her. Pansy and Daisy swooped down and caught the fretful yellow fairy just before she hit the floor.

"Oh, Rose, you really shouldn't frighten us like that," Pansy scolded, mopping Buttercup's brow with her tiny purple handkerchief. She shuddered when she looked at the costumed princess and had to turn away. "Whatever will your parents think?"

That was what Rose wanted to know, too. And what would other people think — people who did not know it was she under the fur? "Sorry, Buttercup," Rose mumbled. She reached down to pat the fairy, but pulled her hand back when the pixies shied away from the fake claws. "Sorry," she repeated.

She *was* sorry, but beneath the disguise her heart was beating fast with excitement. Already she was getting quite a different reaction than she usually did. Her costume was working!

Clomp! Rose lurched toward the stairs noisily. She had to walk with a hitch in her step to keep the too-big boots on. The effect only added to the outfit. As she began her descent down the stairs, she saw her parents waiting for her at the bottom. They were dressed as chess pieces, in all-white angular costumes. The only color they wore were the spots of makeup on their cheeks and lips.

King Hector saw his daughter first and instinctively put his arm around his wife to steady her. When the queen turned, she shrieked loudly. Rose felt certain she'd have bolted from the room had her husband not kept his firm grip.

"Rose, is that you?" King Hector's normally booming voice was almost timid.

"Yes, Father." Rose clomped the rest of the way down the stairs, grinning beneath her mask.

"Darling, what have you done?" the queen whimpered. "Why on earth would you want to hide your wonderful beauty?"

Rose grimaced but did not respond.

"You look so . . . furry," the king told Rose, seeming to search for a compliment.

"Thank you, Father." Rose beamed.

The king patted his daughter gingerly before taking the queen's arm. "Shall we?" He led the family out the door to the waiting coach.

Settled on the red velvet seat across from her parents, Rose sat back and relaxed. She could not help but smile at the way her mother kept glancing at her nervously. She wasn't sure what to expect at the party, but she felt more free than she ever had in her life.

When the pages opened the double doors leading to the Dappers' great hall, Rose had to steady herself on her father's arm with a hairy paw. The grand room was by far the finest she had ever seen, and she shivered with excitement in spite of her warm fur costume.

Silk banners fluttered from the ceiling and curved gracefully around thick carved pillars. Banquet tables laden with decadent pyramids of food and fountains of drinks encircled the room. But even the elaborate displays of food paled in comparison to the bedecked guests. Everyone was clothed head to toe in fanciful, elaborate costumes. It made Rose's head spin. Even if she *could* recognize her friends in their costumes, finding them would be difficult in such a crowd. It looked like the royals from several lands had turned out for the festivities!

Patting her father's arm, Rose excused herself from her parents' side. Standing near them would give away her identity for sure.

"Do be careful, dear!" her mother called out as Rose disappeared into the crowd.

Rose peered into the eyes behind several masks as she made her way down the entry stairs, but none looked familiar. "Looking for a prince?" a young frog asked when she gave him a particularly long look.

"Princess, actually," Rose answered. She did not want to linger. But the frog had smiling eyes.

"Can I hop? I mean, help?" the frog asked, jumping

out of the way of a servant carrying a towering tray of crystal glasses and nearly trodding on Rose's boot. "What is she wearing?"

"That's just it. I don't know," Rose explained. "I don't know what any of them are wearing."

"So you are looking for a pack of princesses," the frog deduced. "Friends or foes?"

"Oh, definitely friends." Rose continued to peer around the room, but she no longer was anxious to ditch the chatty frog. He was fun — in an odd sort of way — and he seemed to like her, even though there was no way he could know that she was Beauty. Rose realized with a start that she liked him, too — and that she had no idea who he was, either.

"Who are you?" she asked bluntly when her curiosity got the best of her.

"Ladies first." The frog bowed slightly and had to use his hands to steady his big, warty head and lift it back to upright.

"But I asked first," Rose argued playfully.

"Beauty before wisdom." The frog sighed in mock defeat. "Or is that the other way around?" He scratched his brow over the fake eyes that bulged over his own kind green ones.

Rose's heart skipped at the word *beauty*. *He knows,* she thought, disappointed. Then she realized he was calling himself more lovely than she. He was only making another joke!

"I think it is *age* before beauty," Rose said. "And by the look of your wrinkles, you must be older than I." Rose poked at the rubbery green material around the frog's neck with one of her claws.

"I don't know if these wrinkles are old, but I can tell you they are hot!" The frog fanned himself with a webbed hand.

Rose nodded in agreement. "This fur hood is none too cool, either," she agreed. "But you are avoiding the question!"

"That I am, Beastie. That I am. In spite of being awkward and warm, I enjoy being hidden in here." The frog stumbled into a chair and sat down with a rubbery squeak. "It is far easier to be a part of the masquerade than to be my true self. I find *that* to be the most difficult task of all, don't you?"

Rose was stunned. She sank into a chair beside the mysterious amphibious prince. He was starting to sound a lot like Lady Bathilde. And he seemed to know exactly what it was like to feel trapped by a reputation that one did not choose. "Indeed," she muttered.

"Now, though the pleasure has been mine, you must excuse me while I hop off for a cooling dip in the lily pond." The frog stood. Rose could tell he was about to bow again, but she stopped him before his head tipped him over.

"It has been *my* pleasure, Sir Toad," she said. "Enjoy your swim."

Rose watched him leave with regret. His big, bowed legs gangled about. Whoever he was, he made a great frog. And, she sensed, a great friend! The frog had really seemed to like the person she was under all of that matted fur. He certainly hadn't befriended her because of her looks! Rose couldn't wait to tell Snow, Ella, and Rapunzel the whole story.

As she stood to resume her search, Rose's boot got caught in her chair. Luckily a purple-scaled arm arrested her fall and before she knew it Rose was looking into the face of a dragon. "May I assist you?" a familiar voice asked.

"The costume is a bit awkward," Rose admitted. "I can't actually see very much from behind this hot mask."

"I know what you mean." The dragon offered his arm, which Rose accepted. "Perhaps we will do better together?" he suggested. "Or perhaps the mysterious beast would like me to fetch her a drink?"

The voice was her first clue, but that last bit of courtesy did it. Rose looked again into the dragon's eyes and felt no doubt. It was Val! How like him to pretend he did not recognize her. "Don't bother yourself, dear dragon. Though you can help me look for a few princesses I'd like to find."

"I'd be happy to. Dragons do like damsels," Val admitted. "Well, most of them." His eyes were locked on a hideous pair of peacocks preening in the corner.

Rose followed his gaze. It was Hagatha and Prunilla, decked out in beautiful plumage! It was clear they had ordered their costumes from the finest tailor in town. Rose shook her scruffy head. The gorgeous feathers only made Ella's ugly stepsisters look even more hideous.

"Their beaks look so real," Val said with wonder. Obviously he really couldn't see much from behind his mask.

"They're not wearing beaks!" Rose laughed so hard it brought tears to her eyes. It was several moments before she was able to peer out of her eyeholes and look again for her friends.

All around her she saw jesters and foxes, magicians and hounds, minstrels and sprites. But she felt certain that none of them was Snow, Ella, or Rapunzel. Where and who could they be?

Chapter Fourteen
A-Hunting We Shall Go

Snow gasped as she entered the hall. This was definitely the place! She ducked around the arm of the page waiting to receive her and waved happily at her seven short escorts. The dwarves had insisted on accompanying her to the party and insisted just as vehemently that they did not want to come inside.

"I'm no highfalutin, crown-toting, jewel-wearing royal —"

Mort interrupted Gruff's tirade. "*Eight* dwarves at the party would be seven too many, dear Snow." Mort chuckled and gently adjusted the pointy hat on Snow's head. "You go on now, and tell us all about it when you come home."

Seven small hands waved back at Snow. Satisfied she was safe, the dwarves turned and held their lanterns high to see their way back to their cottage.

Snow sighed, clapped her hands together, and

spun around to get a better look at the glorious party inside. Her floppy dwarf hat slipped to one side and she quickly put a hand up to catch it, knocking a well-dressed ostrich beside her.

"Pardon me, Sir Bird," Snow chirped. Then she spotted an elaborately costumed bear. "Why, I wasn't expecting to see so many grand animals," she said excitedly. "Please, may I pet your pelt? Just once?"

The bear in the vest seemed taken aback by Snow's enthusiasm but silently offered a paw. Snow stroked it and crooned, "Oh, it's lovely! Now you must excuse me. I need to hunt for my friends. And perhaps some more animals." Snow giggled to herself. "Just imagine. Me. Hunting!" The thought was too silly and kept Snow grinning widely as she searched through the crowd.

There was so much to see, Snow had trouble remembering to stay in character. She had practiced waddling just a little as she walked behind Dim on the way here. He had the most delightful dwarf swagger — the way his chest puffed out and he moved as much from side to side as forward.

Snow side-swaggered her way from one end of the giant hall to the other, stopping every few feet to compliment other partiers on their wonderful masquerade outfits. Every creature under the sun was in the room! But where were her friends?

Snow stopped and pulled her white beard, just like

Mort did when he was thinking. She took a good look around and — there!

Snow spotted a knight, just on the other side of one of the banquet tables. He wore a tall jousting helmet and the visor covered his face. But there was something about the sturdy way he was standing. . . . It had to be. . . but how had she stuffed all her hair into that helmet?

And — there! Right next to the knight but facing the other way was a friendly purple dragon holding out refreshments to an awful, yet oddly delicate-looking beast. There was no doubt in Snow's mind she had spotted Rapunzel, Val, and Rose. But what about Ella?

Snow was making her way through the crowd and keeping her eyes on Rapunzel when the hall doors opened and a new guest fluttered in, all dressed in white.

"Gosh, and I thought *I* was late," Snow said to herself. She hoped the new guest had not had a carriage breakdown!

The tardy guest — a graceful swan — hurried through the doors and plunged into the crowd, swimming right toward Rose and Val. Snow recognized something in that grace, and the late arrival. . . . She felt a smile growing on her face. That swan simply had to be Ella!

Snow felt giddy. The banquet hall, the costumes, the break from studying, and her wonderful friends . . . it was all so perfect.

"Rose, I just want to give you a good scratch behind the ears. Your costume is so cute!" Snow squealed, rushing toward her friends.

Rose scratched her own itchy costume and looked wide-eyed at the dwarf cooing at her. Recognition showed even through all of her fur. "Snow! You look just like your family! But how did you know it was me?" Rose asked.

"By your dainty paws, of course." Snow giggled, unable to resist petting Rose's fur.

"You're Rose?" Val asked. He lifted his dragon head slightly for a better view.

"Of course she's Rose!" a knight with an unusually high voice and a towering helmet proclaimed. "I would know those whiskers anywhere." The knight flicked them with a long sword.

"Rapunzel! You look terrific!" Val laughed. Snow had to agree. She was about to compliment the knight herself when a white swan pecked her gently on the shoulder.

"Oh, Snow, you make a perfect dwarf!" Ella bent her graceful neck into the crowd. "And Rapunzel — the hero!" Ella seemed excited to see her friends. "I hope you don't have plans to capture any damsels tonight — at least not while this fierce knight is watching," she told Val slyly.

Val grinned as he stooped to pick up Ella's fallen feathers. "I thought I recognized these," he said. "And I definitely recognized my sword, and Snow's fair skin. But I had no idea Beauty could look like such a beast!"

"Oh, stop," Rose said. "You knew it was me all along! You all did!" Snow thought Rose sounded pleased that her friends could spot her through her fur. Then the lovely beast's eyes *really* lit up.

"But I *did* meet a frog who had no idea who I was under my costume. And he liked me!"

"Of course he did," Ella said, flapping her wings.

"No, listen," Rose went on, "he *really* didn't recognize me. I'm sure he wasn't pretending." She thumped Val with his own dragon tail. "And he was so friendly!"

"I wasn't pretending," Val moped. "I'm friendly."

"A little too friendly," Rapunzel whispered to the dragon, placing a gloved hand on the hilt of her sword.

Rose was looking around excitedly. "I want you all to meet him. I think we could all be friends."

Snow nodded vigorously. What could be better than a new friend who was a frog? "We'll help you find him," she offered.

Rapunzel lowered her visor and set her shoulders.

"Allow me." She bowed gallantly. "Come on, Dragon."
Val and Rapunzel set off in one direction, leaving Ella,
Snow, and Rose to circle in the other.

"Come on," Snow said, linking one arm with Ella
and one with Rose. "He can't have hopped far!"

Chapter Fifteen
Crash!

"I don't think Rose met a frog at all. I think he must have been a chameleon!" Rapunzel and Val had looked everywhere and still there was no sign of Rose's mysterious new friend. Not that it was dampening Rapunzel's fun. Turning quickly and planting her feet, she drew her sword and pointed it at Val's purple padded chest. "Hold, villain. I challenge thee to a duel!"

"Here. Hold this." Val knocked Rapunzel's sword to the side and pulled off the head of his costume. "I have to take it off before I start breathing fire for real! Is it ever hot in there. Besides, it is a lot easier to see now." Val mopped his brow with a monogrammed handkerchief and looked around the crowded room.

Rapunzel posed with the dragon's head under one arm and her sword planted on the floor beside her. She gazed into the distance. "How do I look?" she asked. "Victorious? Fresh from the fight?"

"Of course, Sir Knight," Val said, sounding a little tired. He snatched back his head. "You look brave and true. Now help me on this frog quest. And while we're at it, I want to find Dap, too. He should be around here somewhere."

"Just look for the spilled punch and tipped tables." Rapunzel laughed as she resheathed her sword.

"Very funny." Val rolled his eyes. "Now be good or I'll make you give me back my outfit."

Just then a heavy banquet table crashed to the floor. Rapunzel whirled. She had only just mentioned a tipping table — but she had been joking!

The heavy table lay on its side. Red punch stained the white tablecloth like blood. Food, plates, and glasses spilled out over the shiny floor. As the startled guests moved away from the mess, Rapunzel saw three girls in witch costumes standing on the far side. Then she spotted three more witches on her right — and a warlock on her left!

I'm glad I didn't come as a witch, she thought. *It would have been most unoriginal.*

"Val, did you get a gander at Hag and Prune?" Rapunzel joked, pointing at two of the more hideous witches. But Val already knew what Rapunzel was just figuring out. Those guests weren't in costume. They weren't invited guests, either. They were real witches!

Before anyone could react, the uninvited witches

and warlocks began wreaking havoc. They toppled tables and tore down tapestries, engulfing guests in the heavy woven fabric. One of them even flew up to swing on the enormous chandelier in the center of the room.

Rapunzel turned and ducked, narrowly avoiding having her helmet snatched off by a low-flying witch.

"Do you want to see my hat trick?" The witch cackled to a friend. She reached down over the crowd again, snatched a floppy green hat off a guest's head, and tossed it into the air.

"Isn't that Snow's hat?" Rapunzel turned to Val, but in the mayhem he'd been shuffled away from her. She could see neither hide nor scale of him in the crowd. And the royals were really starting to panic.

Rapunzel was shoved this way and that as the costumed guests did their best to get away from the crashers' nasty antics. With a dull thunk, Rapunzel's helmet was knocked askew. She couldn't see a thing! And there were so many people pushing in around her, she could not lift either of her arms to fix it.

"Help! I can't see!" Rapunzel's voice echoed in her own ears. *Some hero I turned out to be*, she thought as she groped through the throng.

"This way, dear," a high voice cut through the other noise. Something tugged at the scarf, a hero's favor, she had tied around her neck. She heard something else, too — the beating of fairy wings. "It's far too dan-

gerous in here for young princesses," the voice continued and Rapunzel walked in the direction of the tugging until at last she could bring her arms up and
remove her helmet.

The source of the tugging was one of Rose's fairies —
Petunia! Rapunzel grinned. Rose's fairies could be a
nuisance the way they watched out for Rose every single second. But this time Rapunzel was grateful they'd
been keeping an eye on her, too.

"Thanks. You arrived just in time!" she admitted.

Just beyond the double doors, Rapunzel spotted
Ella, Snow, Rose, and Val, all being corralled by a blur
of color and wings. She started to slow her pace, but
Petunia snagged a long bit of her hair and flew with it
toward the exit. "Come along now!" she squeaked.
"We're not in the clear yet."

Beside the door, Lord and Lady Dapper stood
dumbfounded, looking at the chaos their party had be-
come. Guests were slipping on spilled food. Witches
were circling the ceiling, hoisting drinks, singing silly
spells, and knocking off hats.

"This'll teach you to leave us off your guest list,"
one witch yelled, upending her mug over King Dapper's head.

Rapunzel felt terrible for the royal couple. They
were only trying to get to know their new neighbors!
She tried to pause next to them long enough to bow.

"Good-bye," she said. "Thank you for a lovely even —"
She could not finish her sentence before she was
tugged out the door by her hair.

As the five friends were shepherded into Rose's
family coach, Rapunzel glanced over her shoulder and
winced. Through the open door she saw the enormous
chandelier crash to the ground, spraying crystal everywhere. Out of the din she heard one witch's nasty cackle
above them all. "Welcome to the neighborhood!" The
witch laughed.

Chapter Sixteen

True or False

Rose could not believe the day of exams had actually arrived. She felt like she had been living in a strange slow-motion dream ever since the masquerade. The party had been magical and liberating — just what she had hoped for. But like a dream, it had taken an unexpected turn and left her feeling groggy and confused.

In her head she had gone over and over her conversation with the mysterious frog. Who was he? Had he really not recognized her? How would she know him if they met again, out of costume? She wished yet again that they had found him before the party had ended.

Reaching with her left hand into the velvet-lined pocket of her gown, Rose felt the small patch of fur she had taken from her costume to remind herself of the strange night.

A trumpet blasted and Rose was rudely reminded that the party was over. She was back in school. Back to her old self. The piece of fabric she held in her other hand was not a memento from a strange and wonderful party. It was her Stitchery exam! The girls were supposed to stitch a small flower in the center of their embroidery hoops. And Rose had forgotten all about it while she was daydreaming.

She quickly jabbed in a few stitches. She hadn't finished, but it would have to do. Madame Taffeta was collecting their pieces. Rose shook her head again to clear her mind and caught sight of Snow struggling to take out a row of untidy stitches before Madame Taffeta got to her desk. It was too late. Poor Snow. She was an excellent cook and quite handy with an ax. But she was hopeless with a needle.

Not that my work is much better today, Rose thought. She was distracted and out of practice and her test looked nothing like her usual fine work. *Beauty's work*. Rose scowled.

When the last hoop was collected, Madame Taffeta waved the Bloomers out of the room. Rose thought she looked as dazed and exhausted as her students. The exams were grueling for everyone. The halls had never seemed so quiet between classes before.

The four friends found one another without even trying and walked down the hall together, speaking in whispers.

"That wasn't so bad." Rapunzel leaned in close. "But I'm dreading Looking Glass."

Rose had never heard Rapunzel say she was dreading anything before. She looked at her bold friend with surprise.

"Me too. I stayed up all night last night trying to study." The rings under Ella's eyes showed she was telling the truth. "But now I'm so tired I can't remember a thing! And I'm certain Hagatha and Prunilla are doing poorly."

Rose had to admit she wasn't looking forward to the next test, either. She had meant to do a few practice 'dos the night before but found she couldn't even remember which hairdos she was supposed to be studying! But when the exam was under way she felt worse for Rapunzel. Her long-tressed friend was definitely having a bad-hair day, and her tiara twist turned out looking like a tiara tornado.

When the test was over, Rose sighed into the mirror — all of the back-combing she had been doing had given her split ends. Her hair, too, had seen better days. But even without studying she had done okay.

Madame Spiegel walked around the room inspecting the girls' hair and recording their marks on a scroll. She looked less than thrilled with Ella's twist, which bore a striking resemblance to a coronation knot. And twice her eyebrows lifted — once at Rapunzel's mirror and once at Rose's. Rose could not tell if the look was one of surprise or disappointment. Perhaps it was both.

Watching her friends struggle after they had done their best and studied all they could was making Rose feel terrible. And going into her own exams unprepared didn't feel so great, either.

Maybe I've taken too much for granted, Rose thought. *Maybe I really am lucky to be so blessed.* The guilty twinge in Rose's stomach was starting to feel familiar. *And maybe I don't deserve it.*

When the trumpet sounded at the end of Looking Glass, the four friends made their way down the corridor together again. This time nobody spoke. They didn't have to. Clearly each of them was dreading what came next — the Princesses Past and Present oral exam.

Rose's breath felt shallow. Her heart was hammering and her stomach fluttered as she waited in the plush maroon seat of the auditorium filled with nervous Bloomers.

One by one the girls were called. Each one walked to the front of the room where they stood alone at a podium and answered questions posed by a panel of judges, including Madame Istoria, Madame Garabaldi, and Lady Bathilde herself. The princesses would be graded on poise, speaking ability, and, of course, whether or not their answers were correct.

Rapunzel was first and, watching her walk to the podium, Rose felt even more nervous. Rose could tell the judges were staring at Rapunzel's hair while they fired off their questions, but soon they were distracted by the princess's natural confidence. The more Rapunzel spoke, the more her confidence seemed to build until she was standing as tall as her towering tiara twist and speaking with real authority. Rose felt her pulse race, this time with excitement. Rapunzel was doing well!

Rose started to relax as she watched several of her classmates answer the questions placed before them. Most of them did just fine. *This shouldn't be too difficult*, she told herself.

But when her name was called and she started the long walk to the podium, the fluttering and hammering started all over again.

Rose wiped her damp hands on her skirts as she ascended the stairs. She had never really been nervous before and she didn't much like it. Taking a deep breath, she steadied herself on the podium and looked out at the panel of judges and the audience of Bloomers.

She tried to smile at the judges as she had been taught, to set them and herself at ease. But her face felt frozen, and none of the judges returned the friendly gesture.

"Briar Rose." The first judge, Sir Spondence, frowned slightly at his list of questions. "Your topic today will be moral history, and your first question is this: What can we learn from the story of the princess who would not shut the stable doors?"

Rose gulped. She remembered hearing Madame Istoria assign the story, but she had never actually read it! Suddenly her hands were sweating more than they had when she was inside the beast costume.

"The moral of the story is a simple truth from which we all may benefit," Rose began by stating the obvious. She would have to use her public-speaking skills and charm to muddle through. "If we learn from the famous foibles of princesses past, we can avoid making the same mistakes they've made. We can shut the stable doors on future troubles of the same kind."

There. Nothing she had said was untrue. But it wasn't the right answer, either. She'd simply evaded the question. Rose struggled through her next questions feeling like she was talking in riddles and wishing she were a fourth-year Crown. Riddles and Names was an important part of their coursework.

One look at her friends' faces in the audience and Rose could tell they were as baffled by her answers as she was. Ella looked tired and confused. The concern in her eyes made the circles beneath them even more pronounced. Rapunzel was biting her lips so hard Rose could tell it was all she could do not to stand up on her seat and shout the correct answers. And were those tears of sympathy filling Snow's wide eyes?

Rose had to look away before her own eyes filled up. She was failing!

My gifts have abandoned me, Rose thought. And then an even worse thought entered her head. *I have abandoned my gifts!*

"That is all, Briar Rose. You may step down." Madame Garabaldi did not look up from her scroll as she spoke, but merely waved her hand dismissively.

Rose wanted to protest, to ask for another chance. But she knew she could do no better. Not now, or maybe ever! Looking dumbly out at her classmates, Rose willed her feet to move. All eyes were on her and Rose wondered what they saw. Was this her true self? The very thought made Rose shudder. She certainly hoped not.

Chapter Seventeen

From Bad to Worse

"Do you think she thought the questions were riddles?" Snow whispered as Rose left the podium.

Ella shook her head mutely. She had no idea what to think, or what had just happened. Rose was always so composed, so self-assured, so good at whatever she tried to do. What had gone wrong? As these thoughts raced through Ella's head, Rose descended the stairs, stumbling and nearly tripping on the last one.

"Oh, no!" Snow gasped.

Ella dropped her head in her hands. This day was definitely going from bad to worse.

Exams had been going terribly. During Stitchery she had only needed to sew a basic floral embroidery, something she had done hundreds of times with ease. But she'd accidentally used tapestry floss — left in her bag after she'd tried to teach Hagatha and Prunilla tapestry basics — instead of finer embroidery thread. Tapestry floss was more difficult to handle and Ella's flower had looked like a garden weed. Normally Ella would have recognized her mistake immediately. But she was so exhausted from a week of almost no sleep that she didn't realize what she was doing until it was too late. Madame Taffeta's eyebrows had risen markedly when she'd collected Ella's hoop.

"Tapestry floss?" she'd said, half asking and half taking note. Ella gasped, suddenly aware of what she had done. But the trumpet had sounded, and there was nothing she could do but move on to the next exam.

Looking Glass had gone no better. After combing all of the tangles out of her long blond hair, she'd worked tirelessly to complete her hairdo. But while her thoughts drifted to the recent masquerade, her hands began to create the style she'd shown her stepsisters over and over in the last week — a coronation knot. By the time she had the knot finished, Madame Spiegel was already making her evaluation notes on a large pink scroll.

"Ella, whatever happened to your tiara twist?" she asked, her eyes full of confusion. "You're usually the finest tiara twister in the class."

Ella looked at her reflection in the mirror above the

dressing table and watched her face redden with shame. "I'm not quite sure," she mumbled. She had no hope of passing but she at least hoped Madame Spiegel would not think she was pompous for preparing her hair to receive a larger crown!

"You'll do better in Frog ID," Snow had consoled her on the way to the next exam. "Those froggies just adore you!"

But Ella got so distracted worrying about how her stepsisters were faring in their Tapestry Basics exam, she mistook a large warty frog for a prince and kissed him right in front of Madame Bultad.

"Cinderella!" the teacher had croaked. "Have I not taught you anything this semester?"

"Ribbit," the frog had added his own belched insult.

Ella had wanted to burst into tears. It was all too much. She was doing horribly, and felt certain that Hagatha and Prunilla were, too. She was clearly doomed to a fate too awful to think about.

And now, in Princesses Past and Present, Ella had just watched the normally poised, well-prepared Rose give the strangest answers to her oral moral history questions. She had managed not to fall when she'd tripped on the last step, thank goodness. But it was so unlike Rose to flub something or to stumble at all. It did not give Ella much hope for herself.

"Cinderella Brown," Madame Garibaldi called. "Please take the podium."

Ella stood, walked to the stage, and looked out at the judges.

It's all right, she tried to tell herself. *Just remain focused.* But she was filled with panic.

"Cinderella, your first question is this," Madame Garabaldi began. "What was Princess Atonia Bejewel's fatal mistake, and what should we learn from it?"

Ella smiled feebly at the judges as she searched her brain for the answer. The answer was in there somewhere, if she could only find it! After several long moments of silence she began to speak.

"Princess Bejewel was not honest with her betrothed about the spell that had been cast upon her. When he learned that she did not trust him with the truth, the prince left her. From this we learn that it is always important to be truthful, no matter how difficult it may be," Ella said.

There was a murmur among the judges, and several of them looked surprised by her answer. Madame Garabaldi was shaking her head.

Wasn't that right? Ella had felt sure that Princess Bej —

Oh, no! Ella suddenly thought. *Princess* Felina *Bejewel was the one who was dishonest with her betrothed.*

That was one of the stories she'd read for Hag and Prune's exam. Atonia was Felina's little sister!

Ella cleared her throat to correct herself, but Madame Istoria was already asking another question.

"What was the mistake made by the owner of the turtle that laid the golden eggs?"

Ella tried not to mumble her answer. When she was finished she looked beseechingly at the judges, but once again they appeared to be flummoxed. Oh, bother! She had just told them about the *son* of the man who owned the golden-egg-laying turtle.

Ella was suddenly overtaken by a strange desire to bang her head on the podium. Though it would obviously do nothing to help the poise portion of her mark, it might shake the Robe curriculum right out of her head. There was so much information in there it was impossible to keep it straight!

Madame Garabaldi narrowed her eyes and glided over to Madame Istoria. Leaning over gracefully, she whispered something in the history professor's ear. Madame Istoria nodded. Then Madame Garabaldi approached Lady Bathilde!

Lady Bathilde's cool gaze never left Ella as she listened to whatever it was Madame Garabaldi said.

"One final question, Cinderella," Madame Garabaldi said. "Can you tell me the names of the three Bejewel sisters, beginning with the oldest?"

Ella sighed in relief. She had reviewed the Bejewel family tree with Hag and Prune just the night before. Finally, a question she could answer!

"Yes. Their names were Felina, Antonia, and Cecilia," Ella said, feeling more pleased than she had all day . . . but still she knew that answering that one question correctly would not earn her a passing grade.

Madame Garabaldi nodded knowingly at Madame Istoria.

"That will be all, Cinderella," Madame Istoria said. "Please step down."

Ella held her head high as she moved toward the stairs, but was not able to keep the tears from filling her eyes. By the time she got to her seat, they were spilling down her smooth cheeks.

Chapter Eighteen
Lessons Learned

Rose sat in the darkest, most removed corner of the auditorium. After finishing her oral exam she had to use every ounce of her willpower to stop herself from fleeing the examination chamber altogether. As she took her seat in the final row of velvet seats, she felt certain that nothing could be as dreadful as failing so miserably in front of everyone. Now, though, she knew she had been wrong.

Watching Ella struggle through her exam was even worse. At one point Rose had to clamp both hands over her mouth to keep from crying out loud. The feeling of helplessness was overwhelming. How she wished she could do something to assist her friend! And on the heels of the helplessness came the horrid realization that she *could* have helped Ella. She could have studied with her or helped her with her steps the moment she found out Ella was responsible for their grades, too! Why hadn't she thought of that before? Now, of course, it was too late.

If only I hadn't been so wrapped up in my own troubles, Rose thought. *Where have I been? Who have I been? How could I have let my friend down like this?*

The trumpet blast signaling the end of the test period echoed in the marble corridors, pulling Rose out of her haze. Still, she did not move until the large auditorium was almost empty. Then it was as if she were released from invisible chains that had been holding her back. With a swish of skirts, she rushed from the room to search for Ella and the rest of her friends. There was something she needed to tell them right away!

The trunk-lined castle corridor was a sea of noise. Gone were the whispers. Gone was the nervous tension. The princesses were chattering loudly about the exams, and most of them were smiling with relief. Rose felt an odd pang. She was happy for her schoolmates and longed to celebrate with them. Yet she could not bring herself to look a single one of them in the eye. The disappointment she might see there would be too much and would remind her of the larger disappointment she felt in herself.

"I let them down," Rose whispered. "I let everyone down." Staring at the floor, Rose knew she didn't have a chance of finding her friends in the bustling hall. It would be easier to locate them outside.

Making her way as invisibly as she could toward her own trunk, Rose was stopped in her tracks by a pair of soft beige slippers with crumbs raining down on them.

"Wasn't that exam awful, Beauty?" Gretel asked with her mouth full of gingerbread.

Rose looked up into Gretel's wide blue eyes, but all she could do was nod. She waited for Gretel to say something about how badly Rose had done. But Gretel just stood there munching away on her post-exam treat.

"I was so scared, I was afraid I wouldn't be able to open my mouth at all!" she finally exclaimed, shoving more cookie in.

"That would be impossible for you!" A brown-haired Bloomer walked up to Rose and Gretel. She had her hands behind her back, struggling with something.

"Beauty, can you help me with these stays? They've come loose. How do you get yours to lay flat — and they are always woven so prettily!" the girl complimented.

"I, uh," Rose stammered. She was taken aback. Gretel and the other girl were treating her no differently than they always did. She didn't understand why they were being so kind to her. As she took the ribbons out of the brown-haired girl's hands and began to weave her stays, the truth hit her like a walnut under twenty mattresses. They didn't care that she wasn't perfect. They liked her anyway.

"I get so wrapped up . . ." Rose said, not realizing she was speaking aloud.

"I beg your pardon?" The princess Rose was helping turned her head.

"I mean . . . I get wrapped up every morning. I have help with my stays — from a whole coachload of fairies, actually." Rose smiled. "It's easy to look your best when you always have help."

"Do they help you with your hair, too?" Gretel asked. She eyed Rose's imperfect tiara twist.

"Usually," Rose said with a grimace, "but I've been doing that myself lately."

"I hope you don't mind my saying I liked it better before," Gretel whispered. The other girl nodded.

"Me too," Rose agreed.

"Thanks." The girl gave a tiny curtsy to Rose when she finished the stays.

Rose returned the gesture. She smiled widely and wanted to laugh. She understood now just how wrapped up in herself and ridiculous she had been. She just hoped her friends would understand and forgive her. With her head a little bit higher, she hurried toward the double doors to find them.

Three steps later she was stopped again — this time

111

by a pair of narrow lace-up high-heeled boots with a perfect polish — Madame Garabaldi's. The shame of her exam debacle flooded back, forcing Rose's head lower.

"Rose." The stern teacher stated her name flatly. "You don't seem pleased with your performance today."

Rose shook her head slightly. That was putting it mildly. She hoped Madame Garabaldi would not lecture her for very long because she was not sure she could keep from crying if Madame G. insisted on rubbing the failure in her face. But when Madame Garabaldi spoke again, some of the strictness in her voice was gone.

"There are many lessons to be learned in life, many ways we are tested," she said softly. "We cannot fail unless we fail to learn from our experiences."

Rose felt stunned. She glanced up to make sure it really was Madame Garabaldi standing in front of her and speaking so gently. The straight nose. The no-nonsense look. Yes, it was she. But was that a tiny glimmer of warmth in her eyes?

"High time you looked me in the eye!" Madame Garabaldi nodded and crossed her arms, and the warmth was replaced by her usual cool stare. "Now, tell me where I can find Cinderella Brown. Speak quickly, I haven't time to dally."

Rose gulped and shook her head that she didn't know. She wasn't sure she would tell Madame Garabaldi where Ella was even if she *did* know. The poor girl was probably a puddle somewhere. The last thing she needed was a lecture from Madame Garabaldi. In fact, Rose was sure the only thing Ella needed right then was her friends.

Chapter Nineteen

A Gifted Bunch

Rapunzel grabbed her cloak and slammed her trunk closed for the day. It shut with a satisfying *thunk* and she heaved a sigh of relief. Exams were over!

But as she turned to leave the castle school, Rapunzel realized that while the exams themselves were over, the aftermath they had created was not. If anything, it had just begun.

Poor Ella, Rapunzel thought as she made her way past clusters of elated princesses on her way to the door. She obviously hadn't had a second to study, and it was all Kastrid's fault! That woman made Madame Gothel seem like a fairy godmother. Rapunzel smiled at the thought of Madame Gothel being a fairy godmother. The witch would probably detest the very idea!

Then there was Rose. What was with her? She'd had plenty of time to study and plenty of help from her fairies, too. It wasn't like Rose to blow off her school-work . . . or her friends.

As the Princess School doors opened wide, Rapunzel's mind flicked back to last week, when Rose was messing up her stitching and her hair. Those "mistakes" were intentional. Did she mean to fail the oral exam, too? The question burned in her mind like a tapered candle as Rapunzel shaded her eyes from the sunlight in an effort to spot her friends. There was Snow, leaning over the carved bridge railing and watching the swans below.

Rapunzel hurried up to her friend. As she got closer, she realized that Snow was not only watching the swans, but was talking to them as well. "And then poor Ella gave another incorrect answer," she cried. "It was just awful! Watching Ella and Rose take the exam was far worse than taking it myself."

Rapunzel tried not to smile as she listened to Snow babble to the birds gliding over the water below. "Have you seen Rose and Ella?" she asked.

Snow spun around, clearly startled out of her one-sided conversation. "Why, no!" she replied. "The poor things! I was just telling the swans all about what happened. I wish exam day had never come!" Her dark eyes were full of worry.

The girls were silent as they waited for Rose and Ella to arrive. After a few minutes Rapunzel began to tap her slippered foot impatiently. Then, through the throngs of princesses spilling out of the school, Rose appeared.

"Are you all right?" Snow asked, throwing her arms around Rose's neck. "That must have been just awful for you!"

Rapunzel was not so sweet and didn't wait for Rose to answer Snow's question before posing her own. "Did you do that on purpose?" she blurted, her eyes boring into her friend's. "Did you want to fail that test?"

Rose's cheeks reddened slightly and she shook her head. "No. I just . . ." Rose let out a giant sigh. "Well, the truth is, I didn't think I had to study. I got so worked up about the fairies' gifts that I didn't stop to notice that it's up to me to *use* them."

Rapunzel could tell that Rose felt like a dunce, and her heart went out to her. Being blessed obviously did have its drawbacks. Still, she couldn't help but smile a little.

"Thought you were perfect, huh?" she asked teasingly. "Well, you really shouldn't believe the tales those fairies tell you. You're good, but *nobody's* perfect."

"Oh, really?" Rose replied, raising an eyebrow. Then she and Rapunzel laughed together. "We *all* have gifts that we need to use wisely," Rose said. "I think one of yours is getting right to the point!"

"And Snow here has a way with animals," Rapunzel

said. "Frog ID just wouldn't be as much fun without her."

"And Ella is the hardest worker I know," Rose said. Then her face fell. "Oh, my gosh! I almost forgot. Where is Ella? Madame Garabaldi stopped me in the hall. She was looking for Ella and said she needed to find her right away. I think she's in trouble!"

"Here she comes!" Snow said, pointing to the top of the school steps. Ella had just come through the doors and was rushing down the stairs.

Rapunzel could see that Ella was still terribly upset. Her smooth skin was blotchy, her eyes were ringed in red, and her handkerchief was wet with tears.

"It looks like Madame G. found her already," Rapunzel murmured as Ella stumbled up to them and collapsed into their arms.

"They're going to kick me out!" she sobbed.

Chapter Twenty

Becoming Clear

Rose walked gracefully into hearthroom, the skirts of her sea-foam-green gown swishing quietly around her. As she took her seat, Snow and Rapunzel glanced at her approvingly, and Rose felt certain she knew why. Her gown was clean and pressed, her hair was held back neatly with a pair of flower clips, and there was not a smudge of soup or dirt to be seen on her skin. Rose beamed at her friends. She felt more like herself than she had in weeks.

Still, she was nervous. Nervous about her grades, and even more nervous for Ella. Though she hadn't spoken with Madame Garabaldi when she exited the school yesterday, Ella was positive she was in serious trouble. Now she sat slumped in her seat, her head drooping forward. She looked thoroughly defeated.

I guess all of our pep talks yesterday weren't enough,

Rose thought. She, Snow, and Rapunzel had walked Ella home, telling her over and over that everything would be all right.

"We won't let them kick you out!" Rapunzel had vowed.

But one look at Ella this morning convinced Rose that the girl had been racked with worry all night.

I'll bet Hag and Prune tormented her, too! Rose thought. *The only gift those girls have is for being nasty!*

Rose leaned forward to whisper something comforting to Ella when Madame Garabaldi strode into the room. "Good morning, ladies," she said coolly. Rose searched the teacher's face for a hint about their marks. Was she pleased? Disappointed?

Madame Garabaldi completed scroll call quickly, giving no hint of exam results. Then she set the attendance scroll down on her marble-topped desk and turned to the squirmy princesses. Rose had not seen so much fidgeting since the day a fellow Bloomer had found a pea under her cushions in Looking Glass.

"Overall you did acceptably well on your exams," she announced as she made her way around the classroom, handing out tiny exam-result scrolls. "In the case that you did not, extra assignments have been given to make sure you keep up with the royal curriculum."

"More Stitchery homework!" Rose heard Rapunzel

grumble when she opened her scroll. "Well, at least I did okay on everything else," she added.

"I have to practice my stitching, too!" Snow exclaimed. "I wonder if they'll let me use the dwarves' mending as homework. I have plenty of that!"

Madame Garabaldi was approaching Rose and Ella's aisle. "Though there were a few disappointments," she went on. Rose felt her face grow warm as Madame Garabaldi's stern gaze fell upon her. A moment later she paused next to Rose's desk and handed her a scroll. Rose felt herself squirm slightly but was relieved that Madame Garabaldi was not looking at Ella. In Ella's current state such a glare would be royally devastating.

Rose unfurled her scroll and sighed with relief. She'd passed everything. She hadn't done well, but she'd passed. And extra assignments in Stitchery, Princesses Past and Present, and Looking Glass would not be too terrible.

Behind her, Rose watched Ella shakily unroll her scroll. Her lower lip was beginning to quiver when Madame Garabaldi bent low and began to speak somewhat softly to Ella. Rose strained to hear.

"I wanted to tell you this yesterday, but couldn't find you after exams had ended," the hearthroom teacher said. "You impressed all of your teachers with your knowledge of advanced curriculum." Rose thought she detected an unusual note of excitement in the teacher's voice. "As a result you have been awarded the opportunity to retake your exams in a fortnight."

A giant smile spread across Rose's face and she looked over at Rapunzel and Snow, who were beaming, too.

Ella's jaw dropped in surprise and she let out a tiny sob. This time, Rose was sure, it was from relief. Ella looked up at Rose, her eyes damp with tears of happiness.

"I'll help you study," Rose mouthed as Madame Garabaldi paused next to her desk. She had one more scroll in her hand. Giving her a steely gaze, she handed the scroll to Rose.

Rose braced herself as she unrolled it and began to read.

Briar Rose,

Please come hither to my chambers as soon as you have received your exam marks. I would like to have a private word with you.

Regards,
Headmistress Bathilde

Rerolling the scroll, Rose glanced at her friends, got to her feet, and moved silently toward the door. The walk to the headmistress's chamber felt unusually long.

Lady Bathilde was waiting behind her desk, the door to her chamber partially open.

"Come in, Briar Rose," she said warmly as she gestured to the seat that Rose remembered all too well.

"I have summoned you to discuss your performance on the examinations. Though you did pass, your performance was a poor reflection of your fine abilities."

Sitting silently in her seat, Rose barely heard what the headmistress was saying. Suddenly all of the confusion about who she truly was and wanted to be was gone. Her gifts, no matter how enchanted, couldn't do her any good on their own. And Rose realized she wanted more than anything to use them.

"Do you have anything to say?" Rose heard Lady Bathilde finish.

Rose nodded. "I am so sorry," she began. "I was so worried that people weren't letting me choose who I want to be that I didn't realize that I already was who I want to be. And though I am blessed by the gifts of seven fairies, I see now that those gifts mean nothing if I do not use them to do my best." She smiled broadly at the headmistress. "And that is precisely what I intend to do."

Lady Bathilde beamed. "Then you have learned a far more valuable lesson than any instructor at the school could ever teach you," she said. "May the wisdom of that lesson stay with you always."

Chapter Twenty-one

Truth Be Told

"I'm so relieved that you're not in trouble!" Snow told Rose as the girls descended the Princess School stairs.

"Me too!" Rose agreed. Up ahead she spotted Rapunzel, Dap, and Val. As she stepped off the last Princess School step to greet them, she felt remarkably free. Midterms were over, and so were her concerns about people expecting her to be perfect. She just had one more thing to do . . . apologize to Dap for her behavior when they'd met. Rose waited patiently for a lull in the conversation.

"It was some party," Val was telling Dap, his eyes shining. "But how did you get rid of the witches?"

"Sorry we didn't stick around to help," Rapunzel said sheepishly.

Rose looked at her friends in confusion. Why was Rapunzel apologizing to Dap?

Dap laughed. "We could have used a brave knight!

My parents decided it would be best to invite them to stay. There's no sense in making enemies in our new kingdom, right?"

Rose felt momentarily faint. His parents? Their new kingdom?

"Wait a —"

"Right!" Rapunzel interrupted. "It's always better to coexist peacefully with a witch than to battle her. I learned that firsthand!"

"Those evil types can really shake things up. They were cackling and hanging from chandeliers all night. Well, except for the broken one, of course."

"Hold on!" Rose said. She peered at Dap. "Dap . . . Dapper. You're a Dapper? Why didn't you tell us?"

Dap looked duly embarrassed. "William Dapper." He bowed his head sheepishly. "And well, we didn't exactly get off to a good start," he said, a little nervously. "Then I never had a proper chance to apologize for my unspeakably rude behavior. I should never have made fun of your hair or your nickname. That was not the true me."

Rose gave him a wide smile. "It wasn't the true me, either!"

"Would you care to begin again, Rose?" Dap asked. He bowed lower and stumbled, catching himself at the last second.

Rose was impressed by Dap's apology. He was really quite charming.

"I'd love to," she said sweetly. Then she peered at him thoughtfully. He had kind green eyes; he was certainly clumsy and rather tall. And all that talk about being true . . . it sounded familiar. Rose raised an eyebrow. "But sir, I must protest that you look and sound a bit like a frog I know. Could you be a frog disguised as a prince?" She peered at him knowingly.

"A frog?" he said, feigning innocence.

"A frog!" Val and Rapunzel exclaimed meaningfully.

"Oh!" Snow cried, finally catching on. "You're the little froggy we were searching for before those nasty witches crashed your party!" She clapped her hands excitedly.

"Well, I wouldn't call him little, but everything else sounds about right," Rapunzel said.

"Then that makes you . . . Of course! Your costume was perfectly beastly," Dap told Rose.

Rose grinned. "Why, thank you. I made it myself!"

A fanfare sounded in the distance, and Val tugged on Dap's arm. "I didn't know it was Rose inside that beast, either," Val grumbled. "But we can discuss that at jousting practice, Frog Prince. Come on — we don't want to be late."

"Jousting!" Rapunzel cried, her eyes narrowing with envy as the boys disappeared through the Charm School gate. But a moment later Ella rushed up to them, bursting with news.

"I just overheard Hagatha and Prunilla complaining about their new course schedule," she said, smiling breathlessly. "They did so well on their exams they've been taken out of their remedial classes. They're furious!"

"Ooh! That should keep them busy!" Snow cooed.

"And out of your hair," Rapunzel added with a laugh.

"And give *us* plenty of time to get you ready for your exams." Rose linked her arm through Ella's. "Anybody else want to come to our study session?" she asked.

"I'm afraid I've had enough studying for now," Snow confessed. "I've got to get home and catch up on my baking!"

"And I need to get to work on my jousting moves," Rapunzel said. "The Charm School tournament is only a few weeks away."

"But Rapunzel, you're a girl!" Snow exclaimed, confused. "You can't possibly compete."

"Indeed. But Val will need a highly skilled coach if he's to have a chance at the title." Rapunzel had a glimmer in her eye that Rose recognized. And as she and Ella headed off together, she was sure that if Rapunzel had anything to do with it, they'd all be celebrating a victory at the close of the tournament.